SEAL'S EMBRACE

TAKE NO PRISONERS BOOK #3

ELLE JAMES

TWISTED PAGE INC

SEAL'S EMBRACE

TAKE NO PRISONERS BOOK #3

New York Times & *USA Today*

Bestselling Author

ELLE JAMES

EBOOK ISBN: 978-1-62695-007-8

PRINT ISBN: 978-1-62695-015-3

FROM THE AUTHOR

As a member of the armed forces, we were required to attend an annual briefing on human trafficking. Most people don't realize what a huge issue this is. Every day men, women and children are stolen from their homes and sold into slavery, held captive, tortured, raped and murdered in the business of selling human flesh.

As a concerned citizen and a human being, be aware of your surroundings so that you do not fall victim to these atrocities, and report suspicious behavior. You might save a life.

I'd like to dedicate this book to those people who ferret out the truth and bring the monsters who commit these crimes to justice.

If you've enjoyed this story, please consider taking the time to leave a review on your favorite retail or reader review site. Authors appreciate your thoughts about the books you read and love it when you share them with others.

Escape with...

Elle James aka Myla Jackson

AUTHOR'S NOTE

Enjoy other military books by Elle James

Visit ellejames.com for more titles and release dates
For hot cowboys, visit her alter ego Myla Jackson at
mylajackson.com
and join Elle James and Myla Jackson's Newsletter at
Newsletter

1
___

"Chow will have to wait." Navy SEAL Chief Special Warfare Operator Caesar Sanchez hurried out of the relocatable unit he shared with Declan "Irish" O'Shea at Bagram Airfield in Afghanistan. "I cut my finger and need to have it looked at before infection sets in." He held up the finger. A minuscule cut oozed blood from the tip.

"Isn't that the same finger you cut two days ago?" Irish fell in beside Caesar.

"Yeah. So? No need to go with me. I'll meet you in the mess hall in fifteen." Caesar didn't slow in his hurry to reach the hospital. Air Force Lieutenant Erin McGee had volunteered again to assist at the outpatient clinic that morning and he wanted to see her. Her duties as one of the flight nurses that flew the Critical Care Air Transport missions meant catching her in the hospital was hit-and-miss. He'd gotten word from Fish, their Navy SEAL Corpsman who also volunteered in the clinic, she was there right now helping out.

Irish snorted. "That pretty LT must be there, or you wouldn't be in such a hurry. I'd better tag along to keep you out of trouble."

Caesar pressed his lips into a thin line. "I don't need a babysitter."

"Look, Nacho, the woman isn't that into you."

Stopping in midstride, Caesar slammed an arm across Irish's chest. "What do you know about Lt. McGee?"

Irish eased back a couple inches. "If she wanted to see you, she'd let you know."

"She doesn't yet know that she wants to see me. That's what I'm working on." He resumed his march toward the Craig Joint Theater Field Hospital. "The more she sees me, the more she'll miss me when I'm not there."

"Man, you have it bad." Irish chuckled. "The more you see her, the more she'll be convinced you're a stalker."

"Hell, I just want to see her." Caesar's steps slowed. "I can't get her out of my head."

"There you go thinking with your dick. You're just mad because she's the one woman you haven't charmed out of her panties."

With a frown, Caesar turned a corner between

buildings and crossed Disney Drive to the hospital. "That's not the point. She's special."

"How many times have I heard you say that?" Irish double-timed a couple steps to keep up.

"This time is different," Caesar insisted, his hand fisting at his side.

"Yeah. Heard that one, too." Irish whistled as he walked alongside Caesar.

Why the hell doesn't Irish give up? "Really, I don't need your assistance."

"You're just afraid she'll fall for me instead."

Caesar stopped cold at the entrance to the clinic and narrowed his gaze. "On second thought, maybe you should wait out here for me."

"No way. There's more than one pretty nurse inside that hospital. I came this far, I might as well check them out." He shoved his sleeves up enough the Celtic tattoos on his biceps were clearly visible. The man, like all his teammates, was muscular, with thick arms and thighs from the strenuous training required of Navy SEALs. And like the rest of them, he had tattoos commemorating ops or events that had particular meaning to all team members.

"Fine. Check out the other nurses, just stay out of my way with Lt. McGee." Caesar pushed through the door and entered the clinic. The space teemed with at least a dozen men and women in duty uniforms or PT uniforms. He should have expected the crowd. If

Erin was helping out, they needed the extra pair of hands.

He signed in at the desk. The young woman taking his information batted her eyes and flirted with him the entire time. He barely saw her, his gaze busily searching for Lt. McGee.

The receptionist pouted and asked him to take a seat.

Caesar sat beside Irish and waited his turn, keeping an eye open for his LT. The auburn-haired nurse wouldn't be hard to spot, as soon as she came out from the examination rooms.

"How about that one?" Irish pointed at a blonde wearing an Air Force desert camouflage uniform and boots. Her hair was pulled back in a tight little bun, all strands neatly pinned flat.

Caesar recognized her as the no-nonsense shift supervisor. Young, but tough enough to chew up grunts and spit them out for fun. A smile slipped across his face. "Nice. You should go for her."

"Thanks, man. I think I will." Irish strolled to the desk, wearing his most charming smile.

He was back in less than a minute, his smile forced. "You could have warned me."

Crossing his arms, Caesar gave him a twisted grin. "Why, when I could watch you suffer the wrath of Lt. Baumer. She's as pretty as they come, but her words can cut like a fillet knife."

"I noticed. I think she took off half my ass." Rubbing his buttocks, he turned and faced the woman who'd set him in his place, his eyes narrowing.

Caesar frowned. "Oh, no you don't."

"What?" Irish raised his hands, his expression all innocence.

"I know that look."

"I have no idea what you're talking about."

Lt. Baumer glanced across the room at him, her brows dipping.

Irish gave her a full-on, you-gotta-love-me grin and winked in her direction. "Challenge accepted. Game on."

Shaking his head, Caesar groaned. "Here we go again."

"What?"

"I'm afraid you've met your match with this one."

"One hundred bucks says I'll have her eating out of the palm of my hand by the end of this tour."

"You're on." Caesar stuck out his uninjured hand and the two shook.

"Sanchez," a firm voice called out.

Caesar spun, his pulse ratcheting up as he faced the woman he couldn't get out of his system.

Irish backhanded him in the chest. "I think you've met your match in that one."

By the way Lt. McGee was shaking her pretty red head, Irish might have it right. What Irish didn't realize

5

was just how much Caesar had been working to break down the lady's defenses. "Trust me, at this very moment, she's on the brink of raising the white flag."

"And her skirt?" Irish snorted. "I seriously doubt it. Wanna lay down another bet?"

"Sorry, I have to go. My future awaits." Caesar took off across the floor, his focus on the petite nurse with deep auburn hair and emerald green eyes.

With her full, luscious lips pressed into a thin line, she led him deeper into the clinic to an examination room. All the way down the aisle, Caesar couldn't help but notice the way her hips swayed beneath the flight suit that hugged her body like a tailored glove.

His groin tightened along with his resolve to have this beauty.

"Sit," she ordered, pointing to the examination table.

Caesar hopped up on the table and spread his knees wide. The only way she was getting to that cut finger was to step between them. Still wearing his PT shorts, he realized the mistake that was. With nothing much to hold him back, he tented the shorts in an instant when the door closed to the room and they were alone.

"You really have to stop cutting yourself. This camp is full of all kinds of germs. Keep this up and you might lose that finger altogether." She pulled a gauze pad out of a drawer, alcohol pads and a bandage before she turned and met his gaze, her own green eyes dancing with humor. "And the answer is no." She pressed her lips together.

"How did you know I was about to ask a question? I might really be here to seek aid for my cut finger."

"Uh huh." She shook her head and stepped between his knees. "Two times in the same week is suspicious. Three times cutting the same finger, and that the injuries just happen to be on the same days as I'm volunteering at the clinic, is proof. You're stalking me." She bumped the inside of his thighs with her hips and sucked in a sharp breath, moving back quickly, her cheeks turning a rosy shade of pink.

So, she wasn't immune to his presence. She just needed a little persuasion.

"Lt. McGee, mi amor, I'm crushed." He pressed his uninjured hand to his chest. "Can I help the fact that I'm clumsy and deeply in love? Have coffee with me just once, and I won't bother you again."

"What do you know about love?" She pushed a loose strand of red hair behind her ear, twin flags of pink flying high on her cheekbones. "And I only have two words for you: fraternization and sexual harassment."

Crooking an eyebrow, he grinned. "That's four."

"Yeah, I know, but with you, they all go together." She swiped the alcohol pad across his finger, careful not to sway sideways and touch his thighs.

At the sting, Caesar bit down on his tongue to keep from hissing.

Two seconds later, she had the wound cleaned, and a bandage plastered over it. "There. Your booboo is all better."

Before she could move away, Caesar hopped off the table and captured her wrist. "What do I have to do for you to look at me as other than a patient?" They stood so close, he could feel the heat of her body through the flight suit.

Her free hand rose to his chest, her eyes widened and her breathing grew more ragged. "An act of God?" She wet her lips.

That simple act sent Caesar over the edge of reason and he swooped in to steal a kiss. "Rules be damned." He captured the back of her head, and bent to crush his lips against hers.

For a moment her hand pressed against his chest, then her fingers curled into his T-shirt and her mouth opened on a gasp.

Caesar thrust his tongue through, sliding it along hers in a long, wet caress. She tasted even sweeter than he'd imagined. When he lifted his head, he whispered against her mouth, "Muy precioso."

The lieutenant gazed up into his face, her eyes glazed, her lips parted. Then she blinked and the spell was broken. She glanced down at his hand on her wrist, and her gaze narrowed. "Do you know how wrong this is? Let go."

Immediately, he released her. "For now. I still want to have coffee with you."

"No. It's a bad idea." She eased back a step.

"Are you afraid of me?"

"No. I'm not afraid of you." She turned back to the cabinet, fished something out of a drawer and a bottle out of the cabinet above. "Drop your drawers."

"What?" He frowned. Had he read her wrong? Surely she wasn't going to...not here...anyone could walk in. His heartbeat quickened.

"You heard me." She turned toward him, syringe in hand and fire in her eyes. "Drop 'em."

He held up his hand. "Seriously? You're giving me a shot for a little cut on my finger?"

"No, for three little cuts on your finger." She tilted her head, her brows rising in challenge. "Are you afraid of me?"

He stared at the syringe she wielded like a weapon. "Frankly, yes."

"A little penicillin is good for warding off infection. And you, Special Warfare Operator Sanchez are an infection I can't afford to catch. Turn around and bend over."

God, he loved it when she bossed him around. He could imagine her ordering him to strip in the bedroom. And he would, one slow item of clothing at a time.

With a deep, calming breath, he performed an about face and dropped his shorts enough for her to jab the needle into his buttocks muscle. The pinprick sting was nothing compared to the swat on the ass she gave him next.

"Now, don't waste my time again unless you're really hurt." She held the door open for him and jerked her head to the side. "Go."

"All that for un besito?" He rubbed his butt as he exited the exam room and returned to the waiting room where Irish stood talking to one of the medical technicians.

"All done?" Irish asked.

"Yeah." He rubbed his ass, tenderly.

His friend smiled at the technician and fell in step with Caesar. "Well? How'd it go?"

"I don't want to talk about it." His ass still stung, but no more so than his ego. Lt. Erin McGee had put him firmly in his place, and more or less told him to bug off.

"What's the matter, Nacho? Did the big bad nurse turn you down?" Irish chuckled. "Don't tell me you're giving up?"

"No way."

Irish clapped a hand to his back. "That's the spirit! Come on, let's get some run time in. My mission meter is pinging. I predict we'll be moving out before the night is over."

As soon as they exited the hospital, Caesar and Irish broke into a jog, heading for the perimeter to stretch their legs. They didn't say a word, just ran.

By the time he returned to their quarters, Caesar had come up with a plan to tempt the pretty LT into coffee and more. She'd responded to his kiss, of that he was certain. And where there was smoke, the passion was muy caliente.

After the SEAL left, Erin retreated to the break room for a cup of cool water. Anything to reduce the heat burning inside.

"Crap, crap, crap!" she muttered beneath her breath, tempted to throw the water over her head to reduce the flames Sanchez's kiss had fanned.

"What's wrong?" Lt. Tracy Baumer reached around her for a cup of her own and filled it with water before she faced Erin.

"Nothing." Her cheeks flooded anew with heat and she cursed her inability to tell a lie.

"Yeah. I can see that." Tracy leaned her back against the counter and sipped from the cup, gaze narrowed over its rim. "Does your nothing have anything to do with the hunky SEAL that just left your examination room?"

Erin tensed. Fraternizing with an enlisted man was strictly forbidden. Especially in theater. But damn it, she needed to vent, and Tracy was her closest friend and knew her secrets. "I don't need this."

"Irritation? Flirtation? Frustration?" Tracy said. "Which one?"

"All of the above." With a sigh, she looked up into Tracy's eyes. "I can't lie. I'm attracted to the man."

"Because he's a SEAL?"

"No." She flung her hands in the air. "Yes. Oh, I don't know." She paced to the end of the break room and back. "I know better than to fall for a guy I outrank and especially for an egotistical girl-in-every-port kind of man. Been there, done that, have the scars to prove it."

"You're not in the same branch of service. He's not in your chain of command." Tracy tilted her head. "I don't see your problem."

Was she kidding? "We're deployed here in Afghanistan. You know the rules. No fraternization. Period. Even if I didn't outrank him."

"It happens." Tracy drank from her cup, her gaze following Erin over the rim.

"Yeah, and people get reprimanded." Erin rubbed the bridge of her nose, feeling a tension headache coming on. "Last month a woman was sent home for getting caught sleeping with her supervisor. Now she's out of the Army. Poof!" She snapped her fingers. "Just like that."

Tracy's lips twisted. "She was stupid to get caught."

Erin's eyes widened. "I can't believe you, of all people would condone such behavior."

Tracy grinned. "Women have needs, just like men."

Her chest tightening, Erin's lips thinned. "That's what Matt said."

"Not all men are like Matt."

The sad thing was that Erin wanted to believe her friend, but..."Sanchez is a player."

Tracy planted a fist on her hip. "How do you know?"

"He's too smooth. Too charming," Erin responded, ticking the items off on her fingers. "And all that Spanish is...is...smarmy." Her normal grasp of the English language escaped her when it came to the SEAL. The harder he tried, the weaker she grew.

"I saw Corporal Bradley flirting with him at the front desk." Trace gave her a narrowed glance. "If you don't want him, I'm sure she would take him in a heartbeat."

"See?" Erin flung her hands in the air. "He's a player."

"Ha!" Tracy grinned as if she'd caught Erin at a lie. "That's where you're wrong. He never once looked at her. The entire time he was at the desk, he was searching for you. He's been in here three times and every time, he's only had eyes for you. I know because I watched him."

Erin didn't want to hear it. Everything Tracy was

saying only made it that much harder for her to resist the man, and she was teetering on the brink as it was. "Why were you watching? Are you interested in the SEAL?"

She shrugged. "He's got a great body and it doesn't hurt to look. But no, I'm not interested." Tracy's shoulders relaxed and she gave Erin a soft smile. "You should give him a chance. Not all men are dicks."

Erin snorted. "Right, from the woman who has 'Back Off!' tattooed across her forehead whenever a man comes near. What about the SEAL they call Irish? He seems to have taken a fancy to you."

Tracy crossed her arms over her chest. "I'm not ready to start something new. My divorce was only final two months ago. And this conversation isn't about me."

"No, and I'm sorry. At least I wasn't married to Matt when he cheated on me."

Tracy's lips tightened and she twisted an imaginary ring around her finger as if the weight of her wedding ring was still there. "Yeah, you were lucky to dodge that bullet. Divorce is expensive and emotionally draining." The nurse pushed back her shoulders. "So, what are you doing about this attraction you're feeling?"

Fighting it with every fiber of my being and losing terribly. With a weak smile, Erin raised her hands, palms up. "Nothing. I rotate out of here in two months.

I'm thinking of resigning my commission and finding a job at a clinic somewhere in Virginia."

"And give up flying as part of the team?" Tracy wrapped her arms around Erin and gave her a big hug. "You should give yourself a chance at love, sweetie."

"But I can't see that happening if I'm always flying somewhere. I want to find a man whose feet are firmly on the ground and who isn't gallivanting around the world."

"Picking up a girl at each stop?"

Erin nodded. "Exactly."

"I hear ya, girl." Tracy hugged her again. "In the meantime, a woman has needs. What are you doing about those?"

"I packed my vibrator. And extra batteries. That will be more than enough."

"Uh huh. Right." Tracy's lips quirked. "My vibrator is the single most-used appliance I have and it still isn't enough. If only men were as reliable as a vibrator. All I have to do is keep new batteries around. The silver bullet goes with me everywhere. But it's not warm and doesn't have arms that can wrap around me."

"That's perhaps the one thing I miss most about Matt. He was okay in bed. Nothing to get excited about. And a warm body beats a cold vibrator any day."

Tracy sighed. "Maintaining a relationship when we're deployed as often as we are is too hard."

"I know. And only a special man will accept that you'll be gone."

"Tell me about it. A man who isn't afraid of a woman in uniform. One who is loyal to a fault and always glad to see you when you get home."

Shaking her head, Erin laughed. "We'd probably be better off getting a dog."

"See? It's not just me."

"I know. I'm the pot calling the kettle black."

Tracy's brows furrowed. "Aren't you on call tonight?"

"I am."

A frown wrinkled her forehead and her friend crossed her arms over her chest. "Then why aren't you sleeping?"

"My building is too hot. I can't sleep."

"Well, things are slowing down now and we don't need you on the floor, so get out of here and sleep."

"Why? It's not like we'll be going up. Things have been pretty quiet lately."

Tracy squeezed her eyes shut. "Oh, baby, I hope you didn't just jinx us." She glanced around for a wood surface and knocked on it. "Last time you bet we wouldn't get hit by casualties, we had a mass casualty event when that suicide bomber struck in town."

"Sorry." Erin grimaced. "I don't wish disaster on anyone. The best nights on call are those where we sleep all the way through the shift." Wishing she'd kept her big mouth shut, Erin knocked on the wooden surface of a desk. "Okay, I'm leaving. Maybe I'll read awhile in my bunk. It'll help me calm down and I'll forget that I need to get laid."

Tracy smiled. "If you need to get laid, I know a SEAL who'd be more than happy to accommodate you."

On the way to her quarters, Erin's thoughts pivoted to that SEAL who'd stolen a single kiss. Damn him to hell. If he hadn't managed to catch her off guard, that would never have happened.

Yeah, right.

The devil on her shoulder snorted, telling her that she'd wanted it from the first visit she'd tended him at the sick call clinic. At that time, she hadn't realized he'd cut his finger on purpose. And then he'd done it two more times, which was stupid, and kinda cute at the same time. What moron cut himself just to see a girl?

One Hispanic SEAL named Caesar Sanchez with brown-black hair and eyes so dark they were almost black. Top that with his broad muscular chest and a rash of tattoos across his biceps and shoulder blades, and he had too-hot-to-handle written all over him. He was the kind of man her mother warned her about when she'd first entered the military.

Hadn't she learned not to fall for a man in the military? Captain Matthew Callahan had taught her that much. A larger-than-life F-16 pilot, he'd swooped in, wooed her, taken her to bed while he'd been screwing another woman at a different base. Hell, from what she'd learned later, he had a conquest in every base around the world. She'd just been stupid to fall for his blond good looks and cocky swagger. He hadn't even been all that good in bed, more worried about getting off than making sure she was satisfied.

Navy SEAL Caesar Sanchez would probably be just like that. She hadn't fallen at his feet and drooled all over his tattoos. Therefore, he saw her as a challenge. And her first opportunity to show him she wouldn't fall in with his plan had been when he'd kissed her.

Erin smacked a palm to her forehead. She'd failed that test; she'd given in and responded. But she sure as hell wouldn't fail the next one. Nothing could happen between her and Sanchez. They were in different rank structures, deployed and...well...she'd already been burned once by a cocky lothario. Once burned and all that.

With her resolve strengthened, she left the hospital headed for her quarters on the first floor in the stack of relocatable buildings. Hot and sexually bothered, she slipped out of her flight suit and into shorts and a T-shirt.

Caesar Sanchez had complicated written all over him. After breaking up with Matt, Erin wanted nothing to do with complicated. Still, the SEAL's kiss had been...wow. And the feel of his hard muscles beneath her fingertips had been...well...wow. Her body heated more and she groaned. How was she supposed to relax when sexual tension built inside with no immediate release in sight?

She riffled through a box of personal items and grabbed a novel from the stack she'd brought along. Maybe immersing herself in a book for the afternoon would erase the residual effects of one unsolicited kiss. When she glanced at the cover, she cocked her arm, ready to throw it across the room. The last thing she needed was an erotic romance novel to stir her blood even further.

Yet, she didn't throw it. Instead, she opened the book and read. Talk about stoking the fire.

2

As a SEAL, downtime was overrated. Sitting around, polishing his weapons gave Caesar far too much time to get bored, think and stew over his conversation earlier that day with Lt. Erin McGee. As the day lengthened into the afternoon, he'd worked out twice, ran once and showered, changed into clean shorts and a T-shirt and lay down on his cot.

Some of the guys had gone off to play a game of volleyball. Caesar hadn't been motivated. The heat of the afternoon waned as the sun eased out of the sky sliding slowly behind the hills surrounding the airbase. Too wound up to eat, he pushed to his feet and headed out for another jog. Instead of aiming for the perimeter, he found himself wandering through the buildings, headed for the stack of RLBs Erin had been assigned to.

His heartbeat kicked up a notch when a woman emerged from a door, dressed in PT shorts and a T-shirt, her dark red hair pulled up in a ponytail.

She walked quickly to the edge of the encampment and set off at in an easy jog around the perimeter, inside the wire.

Glad he had on his tennis shoes, Caesar hurried after her, happy for the gift of a chance to be alone with the woman. Slowly closing the distance, he didn't want to scare her. "Erin!" he called out.

Instead of slowing to wait for him, she ran faster, kicking up the pace.

With a chuckle, Caesar sped ahead, catching her easily, falling in step beside her.

"If I'd wanted to run with you..." she panted, "I'd have slowed down." She stopped abruptly and faced him. "What will it take for you to leave me alone?"

"An act of God." He nodded toward the sunset, the beautiful reds and oranges cloaking the hills. "Can we talk?"

"I have to go now." She drew in several deep breaths before she turned and walked.

He ran ahead of her, turned and jogged backward. "I just want to have coffee with you."

She stopped again, planted both hands on her hips and spoke in a dangerously patient tone, "Why can't you take no for an answer?"

He brandished his killer smile. "You intrigue me."

"Well, you don't intrigue me," she said, her brow furrowing. "The word that describes how I feel about you is annoyed."

"I know." He laughed, unperturbed. "I aim to change that opinion."

"You can't." She turned and set off at the pace of a speed walker.

For a few minutes, he walked alongside her in silence, without breathing hard, his long strides making her look like she was running. "Aren't you amazed that no matter how violent the world can be, a sunset can be so beautiful, each as unique and different from the one before?"

Hmm, pretty deep for a SEAL. She could feel herself soften. Not good. "I never thought about it," she lied. She had thought about it. A lot. Especially when trying to get images of the wounded and dying out of her head.

He gripped her hand in his big one and pulled her to a stop, facing the setting sun as it slipped below the hills. When she tried to pull her hand free, she felt his grasp tighten.

God, he was hot. And the longer he held her hand, the harder he made it for her to resist. Already she was leaning toward him. A little more persuasion and she'd be a goner.

"Tell me. The kiss we shared earlier today. Tell me that it did nothing for you, and I'll go away."

He faced her, lifting her hand in both of his, staring into her gorgeous green eyes in the fading light. "Tell me you don't feel anything when I hold your hand in mine and stare down into your eyes."

She opened her mouth to say something, then closed it again, her gaze locked with his, her fingers curling in his palms.

His pulse leaped. When she didn't say anything, Caesar went on. "What I experienced was as magical, beautiful and as warm as the sunset. I can't walk away. Not when I feel the way I do."

She continued to stare into his eyes, chewing on her bottom lip. "I..."

Before she could form another word, he lowered his head and pressed a kiss to her lips.

At first, her mouth remained still, firming into a tight line.

At least she wasn't moving away. Encouraged, Caesar deepened the light kiss, skimming his tongue across the seam between her lips, his hands moving from hers to her arms and around to her back, dropping low to cup her buttocks.

She gasped, her lips parted and her hands pressed against his chest. But not to push him away. Her fingers dug into the soft fabric of his T-shirt, dragging him closer.

He thrust his tongue through her parted lips and teeth and caressed the length of hers, his hands kneading her ass, pulling her closer until his hardening erection nudged against her belly.

Erin's arms slipped up around his neck, her fingers threading through his hair. The kiss that had started out solely from his side turned around and she gave as good as she got, her tennis-shoe-clad foot, sliding up his calf, her crotch scraping across his thigh.

Heat raged through Caesar as he tugged the hem of her T-shirt free of her shorts and slipped his hands beneath to feel the silky smoothness of her skin. He groaned into her mouth, wanting more than just a kiss, more than to feel her body with his fingers. But how much was too much?

Afraid he'd scare her away, he broke off the kiss, removed his hands from beneath her shirt and took hers. "I've wanted to do that since the day we first met."

"We could get in so much trouble for this," she said, leaning her forehead against his. "If anyone were to see us..."

"We're just two people out here, alone in the dark."

"Silhouetted against a unique sunset," she said, her voice flat.

"Know of a better place, where we won't be seen?" he quipped, fully expecting her to tell him to take a hike.

"I do," she said, her eyes widening.

Could he be this lucky? "Where?"

"The back of the supply building."

His pulse slamming hard against his arteries, he smiled down at her. "Let's go."

"Not together." She bit her lip and glanced around. "Meet me there in five minutes."

He nodded and reluctantly let go of her hand. "Five minutes will be forever."

"No, it'll be enough time to put distance between you and me, in case anyone is watching."

Before she could get an arm's length away, he captured her hand and yanked her back into his arms, kissing her hard on the lips, his hand grasping her bottom, pressing her hard against his arousal. "I'll be there. Will you?"

Erin turned and ran back toward camp, her heart racing, her thoughts spinning. What was she doing? The more distance she put between the two of them, the clearer her mind should have become. Instead, all she could think of was getting to the back of the supply building, stripping naked and making love with the sexy SEAL who'd captured and wooed her in the light of a setting sun. Was she insane?

Yes.

Was she crazy enough to go through with their plan?

Yes!

Perhaps by making love to the man, she would get him out of her system, once and for all. Then she wouldn't be constantly frustrated and horny every time he came in with a cut finger.

As a woman who believed in following the rules, she was taking a giant leap out of her comfort zone. If she were caught, she could lose her commission, maybe even be court marshaled.

The danger only made the assignation that much more titillating. Her speed increased, as if she were running from her own demons. By the time she reached the back of the supply building, she was panting hard, her pulse racing and her heart pounding against her ribs.

She couldn't do this. An officer and an enlisted man being together was wrong. Against every rule in the books. And while deployed was ten times worse. Reason returned as she ducked into a corner, hidden by shadows. When Caesar joined her, she'd tell him she'd changed her mind, that she really couldn't go through with it.

Footsteps crunched in the gravel and she held her breath, forming her words in her mind. Ready to tell him just how she felt, she started to step out.

At that moment, an MP strolled by, carrying an M4 rifle and wearing an armored vest and helmet.

Afraid of being caught and questioned, Erin silently sank back into the shadows and waited for the guard to pass.

Not until the MP continued around a corner and

out of sight did Erin release the breath she'd been holding. That had been far too close. She couldn't do this. Couldn't risk her career over a clandestine meeting with a Navy SEAL enlisted man. Heart pounding, she stepped away from her hiding place and ran into a solid wall of muscles.

Caesar gathered her in his arms and pulled her back into the shadows and up against his powerful body.

What had she been about to do?

His lips closed over hers and all coherent thought flew from her mind as she pushed his shirt up over his chest, her hands skimming across his taut skin.

Caesar grabbed the hem of her shirt and yanked it up over her head, dropping it to the ground. As quickly, he unhooked her bra and let it fall onto her shirt. Then he bent and kissed one of her breasts, sucking the nipple into his mouth, nibbling the hardened tip.

Her core heated and she grabbed the back of his head while arching her back, urging him to take more.

He pulled hard, his tongue swirling around her areola.

Erin bit down on her tongue to keep from moaning out loud. If the MP made another pass through the buildings... If he discovered the two of them...

Excitement ratcheted higher and her core flamed.

Caesar hooked his fingers in the elastic of her

shorts and panties, and he dragged them down her legs and over her tennis shoes.

Naked but for her shoes, she felt the warm, desert air caressing her body, followed by Caesar's fingers. Erin closed her eyes and drew in a deep breath, her breasts swelling into the palms of his large, callused hands.

When she reached for him, he grabbed both wrists in one of his hands and pinned them above her head. "Me first," he whispered against her earlobe.

His free hand cupped her cheek and he raised her face. At first, light and tender, he brushed his lips across hers. The pressure increased and she opened to him, her tongue seeking his and finding it, tangling, touching and tasting his minty freshness.

Slowly, he dragged his mouth away, skimmed along the line of her jaw and downward to the pulse beating at the base of her throat. Not pausing for long, he moved lower to take a breast into his mouth, tonguing the tip until it hardened into a tight bud. "You taste amazing," he said.

She tugged against his grip. "Let me."

Holding firm, he refused to let her touch him. "Not yet."

Anxious to join the exploration, she moaned, her body writhing, her center so hot she thought she might spontaneously combust before he got there.

He slid a hand over her belly then lower to the mound of curls covering her sex.

Panting, she thrust her pelvis forward, wanting him to find that narrow strip of flesh, the center of her desire.

Parting her folds, he did, strumming her like an instrument, to be plucked and played until beautiful music filled her body.

Tension built, she twisted her head back and forth. "There. Sweet Jesus, there!" she cried softly.

Letting go of her wrists, he dropped to his knees and spread her folds with his thumbs.

Erin threaded her fingers through his hair, digging them into his scalp.

His tongue slipped into her channel and he swirled around, then dragged it back up to flick her clit.

Her knees wobbled and she moaned, "Holy hell."

In response, he flicked again and again until her world centered around his tongue and the amazing things he was doing to her body. The more he stroked her, the tighter her muscles stretched until one last touch sent her spiraling out of control. Her breath caught and held. When he would have continued his assault, she pulled his hair, forcing him to stop as she rode the wave all the way to the end. No matter how exquisite, the pleasure wasn't enough. She had to have more.

Caesar rose, dragging his hands up her body as he

straightened, sliding over the curve of her thighs, the swell of her hips and the roundness of her breasts, reminding her of the woman she was but tended to forget while wearing a uniform.

God, this was so wrong, but when she ran her hands down his back and under the elastic band of his shorts, she was past reason. His skin smooth, his muscles hard, she couldn't get enough and pushed his shorts far enough down his legs to free that pulsing, stiff, evidence of his desire. "I need you. Inside me. Now," she begged, her breath coming in short gasps, her body shaking with her continued release.

His hands froze and he drew in a deep breath. "I can't."

"What do you mean you can't?" She wanted to wail out loud, but her words came out in a short breathy burst.

Touching his forehead to hers, Caesar smoothed a stray strand of hair behind her ear. "I don't have protection."

Her heart fell to her belly, though her nerves remained stretched taut. "Do you have any STDs?" she asked, her voice more breathless than she could help.

"No. Recent tests were clear and I haven't been with anyone in a long time."

She snorted, her hands cupping his firm, delectable tush. "I find that hard to believe."

He smiled down at her. "It's true. I told you, I'm not

the kind of guy who leaves a girl in every port. Not my style. Plus my mother would whoop my ass."

Her pulse nudging upward, she made a decision a sane woman wouldn't consider. "Just don't come inside me." She dragged her calf up the side of his, rubbing her aroused sex across his thigh.

"Are you sure?"

She kissed him hard on the lips and said, "Please, hurry before I come to my senses."

Caesar lifted her and she wrapped both legs around his waist. Backing her against the wall of the building, he slid into her, her juices slicking the way. Halfway there, he pulled out.

Erin tightened her thighs, digging her shoe heels into his buttocks. "All the way, frogman."

"Aye, aye!" He thrust hard, filling her completely until his balls slapped against her bottom.

Her back pressed against the building, the residual warmth penetrating her naked skin. She sucked in a sharp breath and held it, relishing the full thickness of him inside her. This was what she'd needed, what she'd craved since meeting the SEAL.

Caesar entered her, the walls of her channel clenching around him, holding him as he pulled out to drive in again.

She closed her eyes, her head falling back, her chest rising with each of his thrusts. Fingernails dug into his shoulders and she moaned, long and low. He never knew tennis shoes against his backside could be so damned sexy.

He couldn't believe he was there, making love to this woman, who up until now had run her life strictly by the books. Her ponytail had slipped loose and hung drunkenly down her back, strands of curly auburn hair stirring around her face, emphasizing her wild beauty.

As much as he liked the highly trained and dedicated nurse, he loved this wild and erotic beauty giving herself to him so completely. As he settled into a deep and timeless rhythm, his muscles tensed, he could sense the rise to an incredible orgasm. God, he'd love to stay buried deep inside her through his release, but he couldn't do that. Neither of them were free of commitment. A baby would only make his campaign to woo her more difficult.

If he wanted to be with her forever, he had to show her how much he respected her, as well as how much he loved her body.

Her body tensed, her back arching as his speed increased.

Caesar palmed her breasts, pinching the tips, rolling them between his thumb and forefinger.

Erin squeezed her eyes shut and bit down on her lip, her head tipping back as her body grew rigid with her release.

Dios, she's beautiful.

At the last moment, when he was on the verge of

losing all reason, he pulled free and dropped her feet to the ground. Angling a few inches, he shot his wad to the side.

Her hands curled around him and finished what had started inside her. When he was spent and the tremors slowly subsided, he cupped her cheek and kissed her. "Like I said....you're amazing."

"Ditto." She leaned against him, her naked body fitting him perfectly. "But now that it's over, I have to ask myself, what have I done?"

He tipped up her chin. "You followed your heart."

Erin snorted. "That's not all I followed." For a long moment, she pressed her cheek into his chest, her arms locked around his waist.

Caesar cupped her ass. "I wish we were in a soft bed where I could hold you the rest of the night, and make love to you into the light of the morning, mi amor."

"You know that can't happen," she whispered, her breath warm on his skin.

"Not here. But when we get back to the States."

"Not even then." She shook her head. "What just happened...should not have." She pushed away until his hands dropped to his sides.

Standing in the shadows, her naked body tinted indigo blue, she'd never been more beautiful or desirable. But the hard set of her jaw and the tears welling in her eyes made his stomach knot. He pulled his shorts up over his still-stiff erection, afraid she was about to break his heart.

"We can never let this happen again," she stated, her voice wobbling at the end.

"Erin—" Unable to stop himself, he reached toward her.

But she backed away. "No. Don't touch me. It only makes it harder for me to say this." She bent to gather her clothes, slipping the shorts up her legs and the T-shirt over her head. "What happened here was wrong."

"No, it wasn't." He stepped closer, careful to keep his hands at his sides. "I have no regrets. What we did was true, honest and beautiful."

Her hands dropped to her sides and her shoulders sagged. "And against every rule in the books."

Caesar tilted his head, his eyes stinging, his chest aching with his growing admiration for this woman. If he wasn't mistaken, he was falling for her and that would make their situation so much more difficult. "After what we just shared...you could walk away and never look back?"

"Don't you see?" Her chin jerked up and her eyes flashed. "I have to. You don't really love me. We had sex. Nothing more, nothing less."

He'd had sex with women before. But none had captured his heart like Erin. She was warm, caring and dedicated to her work. "We didn't just have sex. You're wrong."

"Am I?" Her lips twisted. "As soon as you redeploy, you'll forget I exist."

How can she say this? "You don't know what's in my heart." He gripped her arms. "I'm not that kind of guy. I don't want any other woman. I want you."

"I'm sorry." She straightened and stepped free of his hold. "Maybe I don't want you."

Her words stabbed him in the heart. "Do you really mean that?"

She bit her bottom lip and looked away. "Yes."

He didn't believe her for a moment, but he'd let her go this time. She was scared. He could tell by the way she held her hands together to keep them from shaking. This brave nurse, who saved lives and risked coming to a war-torn country to help others, was afraid. Afraid to give her love only to have it thrown away or stomped on. Somehow, he had to convince her he wasn't a player and that he was worth the risk. He wouldn't betray her trust.

Erin wadded her bra and panties in her fist, turned and ran back to her quarters as if the devil himself were chasing her. Blood pounded in her ears. How could she have let the SEAL make love to her? Was she stupid? Did she want to lose her commission?

Back in her RLB, she threw herself onto her bed and cried. Her breasts stung with beard burn and her nipples remained puckered from his tongue teasing and flicking across the tips. Her thighs ached from riding the SEAL and her sex still throbbed from his wide girth stretching her so incredibly tight. She pressed a hand to her throbbing mons her fingers curling around herself and she missed him already. Why did being an officer in the military have to be so hard? Why couldn't she fall for another officer, instead of a SEAL who would probably never be stationed anywhere near her again?

On the other side of that coin, the man was everything a woman could want: brave, strong, romantic. Hell, he'd taken time to show her the sunset and compare her to its beauty. If that wasn't romantic, Erin didn't know what was.

Burying her face in her pillow, she wept for what she couldn't have, and what would never be. They were two very different people, so close, but worlds apart. And she wept even more, knowing he could well be the very best thing that had ever happened in her life.

3
_____

Caesar had just returned to his quarters when Lieutenant Reed Tucker ducked his head in. "We've got a mission. Meet in the ops tent in fifteen."

Irish glanced at him, glowering. "There went my plan for having dinner with Lt. Baumer."

"Like that was going to happen." Caesar grabbed a towel, shucked his tennis shoes and dug his toes into flip-flops. He'd had a similar idea of hanging out by Erin's building and following her to the mess hall at dinner. Anything to spend more time together after their crazy coupling in the shadow of the supply building. He regretted they wouldn't have more time with each other tonight.

But that was the nature of his world. Tonight, they were on Uncle Sam's dime and time.

He hurried to the shower building, ducked beneath the trickle of water and washed off the sweat and dust he'd accumulated on his jog. Not that the cleansing made a difference. By the time he dressed in his uniform and body armor, he was sweating all over again.

"At least we won't be sitting around tonight polishing our weapons." Similarly equipped, Irish slapped his armor-covered chest. "Let's go get some action."

They were the last two to enter the ops building, and they stood at the rear of the room as their commander briefed them on the mission.

"Early this morning, a German convoy was attacked by the Taliban. Two Germans were killed and four were taken hostage." The commander pointed to a position on the map. "Intel just arrived that the soldiers are being held in a small village in the hills north of Fayzabad. Our state department wants us to get them out alive."

He explained the plan, gave them the coordinates, and they collected the weapons they'd need to accomplish the directive.

The men exited the building and headed for the flight line and the waiting helicopters.

As Caesar strode toward the aircraft, he pushed his troubles with Erin to the back of his mind, his thoughts focusing on the mountains and the task he had to complete. He almost didn't feel the hand on his arm until pressure jerked him to the side.

Irish stood beside the path, waiting for the rest of their team to pass before he leaned close to Caesar. "Nacho, you got company." He tipped his head toward the gap between buildings.

Lt. Erin McGee moved in the shadows, wearing the shorts and running shoes she'd had on earlier when they'd made love. Her hands rested on her hips as she paced back and forth.

"Go on, I'll catch up," Caesar said, but he couldn't rip his gaze from her agitated movements.

Irish took off, chuckling. "Lucky dog."

Making sure none of his teammates saw him, he ducked into the shadows and stood in front of the nurse who'd been on his mind all too much lately. "Hey."

"Hey, yourself." She glanced down at her tennis shoes, gnawing at her bottom lip.

The move made Caesar want to do the same.

"I heard you were headed out."

"Yeah." When she didn't say anything, he glanced over his shoulder at the tail end of the group headed for the landing pad. "I have to go."

"I know." Finally, she glanced up. "Even though everything about...you and me...can only be wrong, please come back safely." The last words came out in a rush, and she flung her arms around his neck, pressing her lips against his.

She hadn't put on her bra and he'd bet she wasn't wearing panties. His cock hardened as he pulled her shirt from the waistband of her shorts. He slipped his hands inside and up her naked back. Madre de Dios, she felt so damned wonderful.

He wished he wasn't wearing that damned armored vest so he could feel her breasts smashed against his chest. Instead, he cupped them in his palms, pushing up her shirt to capture one in his mouth. He sucked hard, nibbled the tip and sighed. Madre de Dios, she feels so damn good.

He raised his head and stared down into her eyes. "I have to go."

"I know." She kissed him again.

He kissed her back, long and hard. With his team waiting, he couldn't linger. When he finally set her a few inches away, he leaned his forehead against hers. "This isn't over."

"It has to be," she whispered, trailing a finger along his neck.

"No."

She opened her mouth to argue.

But he pressed his finger to her lips. "Hasta luego." Caesar touched her lips in a brief kiss. "I'll see you later."

He left her standing in the shadows and ran to

catch up to his team, his lips tingling from that kiss. His fingers aching with the memory of her skin against his.

As the moon edged up over the horizon, a dozen SEALs boarded the helicopters piloted by the 160th Night Stalkers and flew north toward the mountains and the reported Taliban stronghold.

The flight was conducted in silence; each man knew what had to be done and conserved his strength for the fight. When they neared the LZ, the pilot signaled to Tuck who then nodded and circled his finger.

While Big Bird checked the magazine on his high-powered sniper rifle and the clip on his nine-millimeter handgun, Caesar nudged Irish, with his boot waking the SEAL from his usual power nap. The man went from out cold to fully functional in a second.

Caesar, along with Irish, Swede and Fish checked their M4A1 rifles with the SOPMOD upgrades, ensuring functionality and sufficient rounds to accomplish their mission. Checking the strap on his helmet and feeling for the Night Vision Goggles on top, he was confident everything was in place.

The team fast-roped to the ground one hill over from the village. They'd hike in from there, steal into the village, free the captives and get the hell out before any alarms could be sounded.

That was the ideal scenario. Invariably, the enemy put up resistance.

The SEALS would be ready. Tuck took the lead, the rest of the team fanning out in a V as they moved up the dry desert hill and hurried over the ridge to the other side.

On a rise with a clear view of the village, Tuck held up his hand to stop their progression. He pushed his NVGs over his eyes and studied the buildings below.

The rest of the team followed suit.

Caesar spotted a man on top of the building over-looking the road leading into the hamlet. He touched Tuck's shoulder and indicated the sniper's position.

Tuck nodded, pointed to Big Bird and then to the roof. He then pointed to Caesar and Irish to take the lead. They would take out the man on the rooftop with Big Bird as backup with protective fire.

Big Bird set up his position, mounted his rifle on a bipod, extending the legs and settled his belly to the ground, pressing an eye to the sight.

Assuming the lead, Caesar hunkered low to the ground and kept as close to the shadows as possible. When he neared the walls of the village, he tossed a pebble out into the road to distract the man on the roof. Then he ran for the wall and pressed his body against the mud and straw stucco. Moving along its base, he worked his way to the back corner, farthest away from the guard on the roof and waited for Irish.

When the six-foot-two man reached him, he cupped his hands. Caesar stepped onto his locked fingers and was lifted up to the top of the wall. Laying flat over the top, he glanced over an empty courtyard. When nothing moved, he reached a hand down to Irish who grasped it and scaled the wall.

Caesar slid over and dropped to the ground on the other side, careful to land softly. He slipped his NVGs in place and hunkered low, looking for movement. After a moment, he pushed the NVGs off his face and approached a ladder on the outside of the structure leading up to the top. Handing his rifle to Irish, he pulled his knife out of the scabbard on his belt and clamped it between his teeth.

One quiet step at a time, he eased up the ladder to the top of the building, and stepped onto the roof.

The sniper sat on his haunches, a rifle in his hands, his head tilted forward. Asleep.

Caesar eased up behind him and reached for the man's head with one hand, his knife in the other.

Before he could grab the man's Lungee turban, the sentry woke with a jerk and swung around his gun.

Caesar kicked the weapon out of his hand.

Crying out, the guard threw himself at Caesar.

Dodging the attack, Caesar yanked him around and locked his arm around his neck, cutting off his air. He held the smaller man off the surface, feet dangling until his struggles ceased. Then he dropped the man to the rooftop, removed the magazine and the bolt from the man's weapon and tucked them into a pocket.

"Rooftop clear," he said into his radio headset, and he hurried back down the ladder to the ground.

Irish nodded toward the door to the structure he'd just descended.

Standing clear of the entrance, Caesar pushed open the door. He fit his NVGs in place and dropped low before peeking around the corner. The room they stepped into was empty except for a sleeping mat in one corner. The only other room was empty, as well.

When Caesar emerged, he saw Tuck and the rest of the team had entered the village.

Caesar, Irish and two others took the left side while Tuck, Sting Ray, Gator, Fish and Dustman checked the buildings on the right. From what their contact had relayed, the men were being held in the center of the village in the largest structure with a rounded top.

Moving quietly through the streets, the team worked their way past several darkened buildings, sticking to the shadows, making little or no sound. As Caesar neared the center building, he stopped and waited for Tuck to come abreast of his position.

Light shone around the edges of the doorway and angry voices sounded inside. A guard squatted near the door, leaning his back against the mud and straw outer wall, an AK-47 lying across his knees. He rocked back and forth as if struggling to stay awake.

Tuck motioned Dustman forward. "Take the guard. Nacho, cover. I'll go in first."

Dustman edged along the base of the wall, his knife in hand.

Caesar raised his rifle to his shoulder and aimed at the guard. If the guard saw Dustman before he reached him, he wouldn't get off a round before Caesar plugged a bullet between his eyes.

Dustman made the corner of the building without being spotted and had just started along the wall toward the guard when a man stepped through the doorway and spoke to the guard in short, clipped tones.

The guard pushed to his feet.

Dustman, already committed, ran the last five steps and plowed into the two men, knocking them to the ground. Swede and Tuck converged and dispatched the two men.

The noise generated in the struggle apparently drew the attention of the men inside. Two men in the Perahan Tunbans, or baggy pants and long shirts, of the region rushed the door, carrying AK-47s. When the first man cleared the doorway, Tuck yanked him to the side.

Swede reached in and pulled the other one out. Both men were killed with a quick slice of a knife across the throat, severing their vocal cords before they could cry out.

Tuck and Swede entered the building followed by Caesar and Irish. Dustman, Fish and the others held back, ready to enter if the going got rough.

They followed the voices down a short hallway and burst into a room, where two Taliban men held up a German soldier between them while another used the butt of his rifle to slam into the prisoner's face. Three other German solders lay on the ground at the center of the room. Several Taliban men sat in a broad circle watching.

Tuck fired, hitting the man holding the gun. The other two dropped the sagging captive and dove toward the sides of the room.

Shots rang out.

"Bleibt unten!" Tuck yelled, warning the Germans to stay down. Not that the soldiers were moving.

From the brief glimpse Caesar got of the prisoners, they'd been beaten to within an inch of their lives, if they were still alive.

Tuck and Swede dove left, firing at the Taliban men on that side of the room. Irish and Caesar dropped, rolled and came up firing at the men on the right.

Highly trained and experienced at close combat, the SEALs eliminated the opposition one by one.

"We have a truck load of trouble a couple miles out, headed our way." Big Bird reported. "Damn. I spot a man running toward them."

"Take him before they see him," Tuck ordered. "Any injuries to the team?"

No one responded.

Tuck nodded. "Good. Grab a German and let's blow this popsicle stand."

Caesar bent to one of the enemy, the scar on the man's cheek triggering an image in his mind of a photograph he'd seen recently. "Hey, I've seen this face." He bent to touch his fingers to the base of the man's throat. "He's alive."

Tuck leaned over the man. "Fuck. That's Hassan Turbani or something like that. He's pretty high up the food chain of Taliban leadership."

"Hassani Turabi." Caesar remembered the name and the picture he'd seen on the Al Jazeera news station. "He's the bastard responsible for the deaths of our six U.S. soldiers that were paraded before the cameras and then beheaded last fall."

Irish pressed his rifle muzzle to the man's head. "The son of a bitch needs to die."

Tuck's hand shot out. "Wait. They still have four U.S Army captives hidden away somewhere in the hills. He might know where. Bring him along."

"I'm not carrying him," Irish said, lifting one of the Germans in a fireman carry. "After what he did to our guys and these Germans…"

"Shooting him would be too easy," Swede said, his jaw clenched.

"Save him for our intel folks," Tuck insisted. "Our soldiers need every chance we can give them."

Though the action went against everything he stood for, Caesar threw the man over his shoulder and headed for the door. They had to get out of the village before the truckload of Taliban got there first.

Dustman entered the building and collected the fourth German. Dead or alive, they had to get them out.

The five men emerged from the building to the sound of gunfire.

"Sniper on that rooftop." Fish pointed to a spot where tracer rounds lit up the night. Bullets hit the dirt at their feet, encouraging them to move faster. "Gator's on him."

A moment later, the gunfire stopped and Gator ran to catch up to them. With Fish, Sting Ray, Hank and Gator covering for them, the team made it to the entrance to the village.

"Tuck, I've got your back, there have to be fifteen or twenty of them loaded into the back of that pickup," Big Bird said. "And I didn't bring my rocket launcher."

The men ran with sluggish steps, hampered by the dead weight of five injured people.

"Holy shit! They have an RPG! Get down." Big Bird shouted into their headsets.

As one, they dropped to the ground, Caesar and Sting Ray bringing up the rear.

A round slammed into the ground behind them, the explosion rocking the earth.

Shards of shrapnel pierced the air and something ripped into Caesar's lower back, buttocks and thigh, a momentary flash of heat.

"Go, go, go!" Tuck shouted. "Before he loads another round."

Caesar staggered to his feet, and looked over his shoulder where Sting Ray had been. He lay on the ground, moaning, his hand pressed to his side. "Sting Ray's been hit!" He started to throw the Taliban man on the ground, but Dustman beat him to Sting Ray, looped the man's arm over his shoulder and half dragged, half-carried the man up the hill.

Caesar pushed on, his legs wobbling beneath him as he climbed the hill.

Just a little farther.

His mind focused on making the helicopter, images of Erin popped up in him thoughts, a reminder of all he had to live for, all he had waiting for him to return to camp.

Just a little farther.

The men topped the hill and let gravity hurry them down the other side to where the helicopters had landed.

A few feet from the chopper, Caesar's left leg gave out, he dropped the Taliban leader and crashed to the ground, face first. The jolt made him see stars and gray fog settled around the edges of his vision. He tried to rise, but his legs wouldn't cooperate.

Tuck and the other men loaded the Germans on board the helicopters.

"Wait," Caesar tried to cry out over the noise of the engines and blades thumping the air. His voice was weak, his body weaker. If they couldn't hear him and if each person thought he'd gotten on the other craft, they wouldn't know they'd left him behind until too late.

Again, he tried to get his feet under him but his muscles wouldn't move. Twenty yards, that's all he needed. Twenty yards and he'd be on one of the choppers.

One of the helicopters lifted off, hugging the nap of the earth, and swept away.

Caesar clawed at the ground, inching himself toward the remaining chopper. At the rate he was moving, the chopper would leave before he got there.

4

His legs basically useless, Caesar gritted his teeth and focused on crawling to the helicopter, dragging himself along the rocky ground, one agonizing foot at a time. Movement to his rear made him look back at the silhouette of a large man carrying a rifle on a bipod. Pain stabbed through him like a red-hot poker, blinding him. When his vision cleared, he focused on the big man standing beside him.

Big Bird leaned over him. "Nacho, you need a hand?"

Relief flooded him and Caesar nearly wept for joy. "I could."

The big man flung his weapon over his back. "Got a man down out here," he said into the headset. "Make that two." Big Bird scooped Caesar up in his arms and carried him to the chopper, laying him out on the floor of the craft beside an injured German.

As soon as his backside touched the floor, he experienced excruciating agony. When he tried to roll over, he nearly blacked out. He ground his teeth, forced himself to his side and lay still until the dizziness receded. His lower back, buttocks and thigh went numb. Thankful the pain had disappeared, he didn't think beyond that, just concentrated on breathing.

Dustman loaded the Taliban leader into the same craft, none too gently.

"Gotta go!" the pilot yelled.

From the corner of his eye, Caesar caught a glimpse of the truck full of Taliban. The vehicle had stopped and the men on board had all jumped down and ran toward the Blackhawk helicopter, firing their weapons.

The helicopter shuddered and then lifted off the ground. Within seconds, they were high in the sky, well out of range of small arms fire.

As the corpsman, Fish went to work on the wounds he could see and treat. The noise of the aircraft drowned out anything he might have said. When he got to Caesar, he rolled him over and grimaced. "Can't help you there, buddy. The surgeons will have to pick out the pieces. At least you're not bleeding like a stuck pig. Want something for the pain?"

"No. Take care of Sting Ray." Caesar didn't bother

to tell him that he was feeling no pain. Like Fish said, not much they could do in the back of the helicopter.

"Sting Ray is coming around. He's got a few bits of shrapnel embedded in his skin, but he'll be okay."

"Anyone else?" Caesar asked.

"No, we're all accounted for and alive. The Germans are in bad shape. We're lucky we got them out when we did or we'd have been carrying them out in body bags."

Knowing his team was okay, Caesar relaxed and closed his eyes, the roar of the engine lulling him to sleep.

The flight back was the longest and shortest flight Caesar could ever recall. Floating in and out of consciousness, he tried not to worry about the lack of feeling or the fact he couldn't move his legs, preferring to succumb to blessed sleep.

Caesar didn't wake until the craft landed with a jolt on the tarmac at Bagram Airfield. Ambulances stood in a line, medics, hospital staff and volunteers converged on them as soon as the skids touched down.

The Taliban leader was last in and first out, loaded onto a backboard and transported to a waiting ambulance. When they came for Caesar, Fish stepped into their paths.

"Load him on his side, he's got shrapnel wounds to the back, buttocks and thighs. Possible damage to the spinal cord."

At those two words, Caesar's heart skipped several beats and plunged to his belly. Spinal cord injury could lead to paralysis. Was that why he couldn't feel his legs? He prayed they were wrong and wished for the pain to return. Pain meant you were still alive and able to feel.

As they maneuvered him onto a backboard on his side, the little bit of movement jolted something loose and pain ripped through his body. He moaned, biting down hard on his tongue to keep from crying out.

They settled him onto a litter and four volunteers carried him across the tarmac to a waiting ambulance.

"Caesar?" a familiar voice called out to him. Lt. McGee's face appeared over him, her auburn brows knit in a worried frown. "Hey."

"Hey," he managed, the pain radiating through him like a white-hot poker being pressed against his nerves.

"We'll get you fixed up, don't you worry." She squeezed his hand and moved out of the way while he was loaded into the ambulance, then she climbed in beside him, checked his pulse and blood pressure. "Talk to me."

"No." He clamped his jaw against another wave of pain.

"Okay, then I'll talk to you." She went on to talk like they were sitting over a cup of coffee in the mess tent, all the while her hands moved over him, establishing an IV drip. "Do you like dogs? I do. One of these days I hope to have two golden retrievers. Of course, it'll have to be when I'm no longer flying CCATT missions." She leaned down and smiled. "Are you a sports fan? I have to admit, I'm a sucker for a good hockey game. I like the violence and the passion. I know, I'm supposed to be a peace-loving nurse, but give me a fight in the hockey rink and I'm on fire." She chuckled, the sound forced, the worried frown never leaving her brow. "What's your pain level on a scale of one to ten?"

At that particular moment, he was back to no feeling. "Zero."

The V of her brows deepened and she reached out to touch his leg. "Feel that?"

She'd touched him? He shook his head. "No."

"When they were loading you onto the backboard, you were moaning."

"Pain level was at eleven then."

"And nothing now?"

"Nothing."

"Okay. Could be shrapnel pressing against the spinal cord. We'll get you into X-ray and check it out." She gripped his hand and held it the rest of the way to the field hospital.

Being unloaded from the ambulance, the shift once again triggered the pain. He clenched his fists and grunted.

"Hurt?" Erin asked. "That's a good sign."

"Doesn't feel so good," he said through clenched teeth.

"We'll get you on some morphine as soon as possible." Erin leaned over him and whispered in his ear, "I'll see you in a little while." She brushed a chaste kiss across his temple and released his hand.

He was wheeled into the hospital and straight into surgery. Once the anesthesiologist fitted the mask over his face, he was out, his last thought before he drifted off was to send a prayer to God that he would wake up still possessing the ability to walk.

Erin didn't have time to worry about Caesar in surgery. As soon as she got to the hospital, she was ordered to report to the C-17 that had landed an hour earlier and prep it for litters and patients. The state department wanted the Germans transported back to Germany as soon as they'd been stabilized.

She worked beside the other members of her team and the cargo master to transform the cargo area of the big plane into a fully-functional flying ambulance and intensive care unit. Equipment was moved on board, latched down and powered up, with technicians testing the functionality.

While the surgeons operated and did what they could, the CCATT teams worked the inside of the aircraft. Hours later, they were given the word that the patients were ready for transport. The team and every volunteer they could muster moved patients from the hospital to the staging facility, disconnecting respiratory equipment from fixed units to mobile units and moving the patients and the apparatus to the airplane.

When another team brought the SEAL on board, Erin's belly flipped and she hurried to his side to ensure he was carefully placed where she could keep watch over him, as well as two Germans. The other team would care for the other two Germans and the Taliban leader. The German government had balked at allowing the Taliban leader on German soil at Landstuhl. But the American state department insisted he get medical treatment necessary to keep him alive for interrogation purposes. As a trade for rescuing the German soldiers and delivering them home, the intel that hopefully could be gained from Hassani would guide them to the whereabouts of the four Americans still being held.

Erin monitored her patients, checking vital signs. They all slept through the take off.

The flight would be long from Bagram to Germany and she'd be on her feet the entire time. Her job was to get these boys home.

She read Caesar's chart. The surgeon's notes had been brief. He'd removed all but one piece of shrapnel. That one, he'd saved for the surgeon at Landstuhl, who was known for his delicate work with spinal cord injuries.

Erin gazed down at the big SEAL. All the muscles

in the world would be useless if the damage to his spinal cord was permanent. Her heart always bled for the soldiers who made it back to the states crippled for life. What a difference from the young men who'd walked into the war on two feet.

"Hey, no sad faces," a voice whispered, pulling her out of her melancholy.

Her heart warmed and she touched his arm. "You're supposed to be sleeping."

"Thirsty." He smacked parched lips and winked. "I was dreaming about one short, hot drink of water."

"That phrase only works with long cool drinks of water." She got him a cup of water and held up a straw to his lips. "Go slow."

"What's the prognosis?"

"They removed most of the shrapnel."

"Most?"

"You'll have to see a surgeon when we get to Landstuhl to get the last one."

"I take it, that one's lodged close to my spine?" He closed his eyes, his brows creased.

"That's the one. Are you feeling the pain again?"

"A little."

"Yeah. There are no heroes where pain is concerned." She reached for his IV. "I can give you more morphine."

He grabbed her wrist. "Rather have a kiss."

She laughed. Soldiers on pain drugs often asked

her for a kiss. But she'd never wanted to give any of them one. Until now. "All I can do for you is morphine."

"Then I'll wait until we're alone."

"That will be a while."

"I can be a very patient patient. Pardon the pun." He chuckled at his own joke, his frown deepening. "Remind me not to laugh."

"Don't laugh," she said and dipped a cloth in cool water, dabbing it over his forehead and cheeks. "I have to check on my other patients."

"Don't be kissing on them, now."

She smiled. "I promise I won't." His play at jealousy made her warm all over in the cool interior of the aircraft. Moving between respiratory equipment and IV drips, she checked the Germans' vital signs for the sixth time since they'd taken off. Unlike the SEAL, they were fast asleep, sedated, their faces bruised and swollen from torture by the Taliban. She had a hard time forgiving the enemy in the litter near the rear of the plane and was glad she didn't have to treat him. If she was assigned to, she would. But she didn't have to like it.

After she'd done due diligence for the German soldiers, she returned to Caesar's side and offered him another sip of water.

He took it gladly. "I'd rather have that coffee I mentioned back at Bagram."

"When you're up and moving again, I'll consider it."

He braced his hands on the litter, his muscles bunching.

Heart fluttering, Erin placed her hand on his shoulder. "Be still. The more you move now, the more chance of permanently paralyzing yourself."

"Want that coffee," he grunted.

"I'll get you a cup as soon as you're out of surgery and the doctor okays it. I promise."

"I figured you'd be right back on the plane once we land."

"I'll see if I can pull some strings." She checked the tube leading from the fluid bag to his arm. "You should sleep. I'm increasing your sedative."

He reached for her wrist. His grip held surprising strength for someone who'd just been in surgery. "What did I tell you about moving?" she chastised him.

"I want you to know I have no regrets. What we have means something."

Her cheeks burned. Erin avoided his gaze, stared down at where his big hand held her small wrist and she shrugged. "Don't make too much of everything."

"You wouldn't have come to see me off if it meant nothing."

How did she relate her premonition? "I had to see you again. I got that bad feeling that something wasn't right. I couldn't explain it, but I had to see you before you left."

"Did you think I wasn't coming back?"

Her throat closed and the backs of her eyes burned. She nodded.

Caesar snorted. "After that kiss, nothing would keep me away."

She glanced around to see if anyone else was listening to their conversation. The respiratory therapist talked with the flight surgeon on the other side of the German patient. For all intents and purposes, she and Caesar were alone. "The kiss didn't mean anything."

"If it didn't mean anything, you wouldn't have given it to me." He smiled. "The beauty is that you can't take it back." His fingers tightened on her wrist. "I'll get better soon and I'll want another, mi amor."

"That can't happen. You're an enlisted SEAL. I'm an Air Force officer. It won't work."

"You're a woman, I'm a man." His words slowed. "We were meant for each other."

He loosened his grip and smiled, his eyes closing for a moment. "Besides, I liked the way your lips felt on mine. I'll dream about them."

She pulled up the sheet and blanket around him. "You do that." In the meantime, she'd stand watch and make sure he made it to Landstuhl alive. Hopefully, once there he'd get the attention he deserved to save his legs from paralysis. Then maybe she would kiss him again. In private. Away from prying eyes and commanding officers bent on enforcing regulations.

Caesar woke once more as they offloaded the patients at their destination at Ramstein Air Force Base. He was loaded into an ambulance and transported to Landstuhl Regional Medical Center where a surgical staff awaited his arrival. He didn't see Erin again and he really wished he'd had the chance to see her one more time as a whole man. If he came out of surgery paralyzed for life, he wasn't sure what he'd do. He sure as hell wouldn't expect her to hang around a cripple. He wouldn't wish that kind of life on any woman.

As he was wheeled into the operating room, he looked up at the surgical team and smiled. "Do your magic. I plan on walking out of this hospital."

The surgeon nodded, his eyes serious over the surgical mask he wore. He tilted his head toward the anesthesiologist and a mask was pressed to Caesar's face.

Within seconds, his world went black.

Hours, maybe days later, he struggled to wake, a voice calling his name, nagging him to open his eyes. "Can't a guy get a nap around here?" he grumbled.

"Sure, after you prove you're alive and well. Wake up for a minute, and you can go back to sleep."

Soft laughter warmed his insides. He opened one

eye. The light shining from the overhead fixture formed a halo around the red-haired angel bending over him. His other eye gladly opened. "Ah, mi amor." He smiled up at Erin. "What are you doing in the operating room?"

"I'm not in the operating room." She still wore the same clothes as the flight from Bagram and she had dark circles beneath her eyes. "You're in recovery."

He stared up at the ceiling, which meant he was lying on his back. "I take it they got the last piece of shrapnel?"

"They did." She held up a small, clear plastic vial with a tiny metal shard inside. "They saved it for you. A souvenir of your mission."

"Fuck the souvenir." He pushed up on his elbows and glanced down at his feet.

"Go ahead. Move them." Eyebrows raised, she grinned.

He concentrated on his toes first, his brain sending a message to his right foot to wiggle them. His right toes wiggled.

A huge weight lifted from his shoulders and he lay back, laughing. "Thank God."

"The doc said you might have a little swelling that could interfere with your spinal cord and may cause some temporary paralysis, but he predicts a full recovery."

"How long? Days, weeks, or months of therapy?"

"Days." She waved toward his legs. "Try moving your leg."

He bent his knee, the effort harder than usual, but he could perform the action.

"You're still suffering the effects of the anesthetics and pain meds. When they've worn off and you're rested, you'll be able to get out of bed and move around with assistance."

He let his knee straighten and he stared up at the ceiling, grinning.

"Thought you might be happy about that," Erin said.

"I'll be even happier when I'm standing on my own two feet, holding you in my arms."

A frown wrinkled her brow and she shook her head. "I told you, that isn't likely to happen again."

He eased up on his elbows again. "The standing or the holding?"

"The standing, yes. Holding?" Her cheeks flushed with color. "Not happening. I promised coffee. Nothing else."

"Bella dama. You present a challenge."

Her lips firmed. "I'm not a game or a conquest."

"No game, mi amor. But a challenge, nonetheless."

"I'm leaving now."

"How soon until you have to be back at Bagram?"

"I'm staying for the next three days. They're short-handed in the ICU, and I'll be helping out on the nightshift."

"Good. We're on for coffee tomorrow morning when you get off duty."

She narrowed her gaze. "Only if you can get up on your own by then. I wouldn't push it. Talk to the doctor when he stops by and see if he's comfortable with you moving around so soon after surgery."

"I'm feeling better already." He started to swing his legs over the side of the bed.

"Seriously?" She laid a hand on his shoulder. "If I have to, I'll have them sedate you. You have to give yourself time to recover. Surgery always entails a bit of inflammation and swelling. And you don't want to pull out the stitches."

"Fine. I'll wait until the doc gives me the okay. But that better be by morning. I'll have my morning coffee with you, if doing so kills me."

"Let's not take it that far. I'd rather delay coffee for a few days than have you die."

A dull roar came from the television set mounted on the wall in the corner of the room.

Caesar glanced at the screen. A mob of people gathered around the gate of what looked like a military base. Squinting, he read the name on the gate. Ramstein. "Did I miss anything while I was out?"

Erin lifted the remote and clicked the mute button. "The Germans are angry we have the Taliban leader responsible for the torture and deaths of their soldiers. They want us to hand his head over on a platter or send him out and let them deal with him."

His fist clenched. "I don't blame them. We walked in on them smashing a prisoner's face. With the butt of a rifle."

Erin nodded. "The soldier you're talking about was transferred to a German hospital. From what little information we got, he's struggling to survive. The damage to his face and throat will take a lot of surgeries to repair. If he survives."

"You got him here?"

"Barely. It was touch and go for a while. The other CCAT team worked hard on the flight over to keep his heart going."

"That Taliban bastard deserves to die a painful death," Caesar said. "He doesn't deserve the best medical care the U.S. has to offer."

"I agree." She stared at the mob on the screen, shaking her head. "But if there's a chance of getting intel from him, we might save other American lives."

Caesar jerked his chin at the screen. "What's going on out there?"

"A couple hundred Germans are lined up at the gate, protesting. Their numbers have been growing since the television station broadcast the news earlier today."

"Great. Just what we need. A riot at the hospital."

Caesar pushed a hand through his hair, wishing he could get into a shower and clean the desert sand off his skin and scalp.

"You can't worry about it. The military police will keep them at bay." Erin returned to his bedside, checked his IV drip and fluffed his pillow.

Unwilling to let her move away, he cupped the back of her neck and pulled her downward.

"Caesar, you shouldn't be moving so much."

"Then stop resisting." He brought her closer until their lips were less than an inch apart. "You know you want to kiss me."

"No, I don't," she whispered, her breath puffing against his lips. Then she leaned forward and brushed her mouth across his. "Get some sleep."

His lips heated from her touch. "Only if you get some too."

"I plan on it. They've set aside a room with a bed and a shower I get to use for the next eight hours. I'm on duty tonight at eleven."

"You need more sleep than that."

"I'll be fine." She straightened. "As long as I leave now. I'll see you for coffee in the morning."

"Count on it." Caesar waited until the door to his room closed behind her before he laid back and closed his eyes. After a deep breath, he opened them again, lifted his head and moved his toes again.

Satisfied his legs were working as they should, he

slipped into a troubled sleep. Twice during the day, a nurse entered the room, checked his vitals, drawing blood once and generally waking him. He knew sleep was the best cure for his body and he forced himself to close his eyes each time, when he'd rather get up and find Erin and crawl in bed by her side. His mind groggy with drugs and sleep, he had enough sense to remind himself that Erin was worth taking it slow. He didn't want to scare her off.

5
———

Thankfully, a bus ran twenty-four/seven between the hospital and her assigned lodging. Any other day, she'd have walked the short distance, but Erin was tired and more than ready to sleep. She checked in at the desk and trudged up to her room.

Exhausted from being on her feet for over twenty hours, Erin showered quickly, slipped into a T-shirt and shorts and climbed into the bed. As she pulled up the sheet and blanket over her shoulders, she registered the echoes of the crowd chanting and shouting outside the gate, making falling to sleep immediately difficult.

Photographs of the injured German soldiers had circulated on the news, igniting anger and a powerful thirst for justice. The people outside wanted to exact their pound of flesh from the Taliban leader.

Forcing the angry mob and their chants and shouts to the back of her mind, Erin closed her eyes and remembered the way Caesar's hands felt on her body, the way he'd made love to her wildly, passionately, ensuring she was as satisfied as he was.

Everything about her attraction to the SEAL was wrong. Granted, they weren't in the same chain of command, and they weren't even in the same branch of service. Still, he was enlisted and she was an officer. She loved her job. Loved that she helped soldiers make it home alive. If she lost her commission, she'd be out of the military.

Her lips still tingled from their kiss and she burned with the aching need to repeat what they'd shared behind the supply building at Bagram, her desire pushing her beyond reason. God, what was she doing to herself? If she had a lick of sense, she'd have gotten on the next flight back to Bagram and forgotten about Caesar and the way he made her want to ignore all the rules.

He was a goddamn SEAL, for heaven's sake! He'd charm his way into her panties with his muscles and tattoos and as soon as he was reassigned, maybe sooner, he'd be on to the next girl. Adrenaline junkies like SEALs and pilots were notorious for multiple affairs and real commitment issues.

So? Why couldn't she let herself enjoy the forbidden? They weren't in Afghanistan. If they happened to kiss and make love in Germany, their actions wouldn't be completely against the rules. Again, he wasn't in her chain of command. For an officer and an enlisted man to hook up wasn't completely unusual.

Despite being bone-tired, Erin tossed and turned until she finally fell into an exhausted sleep. The alarm on her watch woke her six hours later. She clawed her way out of the sleep coma and struggled upright. She'd promised to help out in ICU over the graveyard shift. She'd deployed from Landstuhl, so her credentials were up to date with the hospital, and they needed her to help out. They were short two ICU nurses and another had called in sick earlier that day.

With a sigh, she pushed back the covers and got out of the bed. With only twenty minutes until she went on duty, she didn't have time to stop by Caesar's room. She'd have to wait until morning and the promised cup of coffee. With quick, efficient strokes, she brushed back her hair into a tight bun at the nape of her neck, pinned the loose strands in place and shook the wrinkles out of the clean flight suit she'd brought on board the C-17 in her backpack. After dressing quickly, she laced her boots and headed for the hospital and the Intensive Care Unit.

Shift change took place and she was assigned to two patients. One of them was the Taliban leader,

Hassani Nurabi. She had to push aside her loathing of all he represented to provide for his care, telling herself he was just another human being, not a monster that should be destroyed. And if any possibility existed of getting information out of him to locate and rescue the four Americans, he could be worth saving.

The night dragged on. Thankfully, her patients remained stable and other than changing IV bags, administering medications, checking drainage tubes and vital signs, the shift was uneventful. She met with the nurses at the nurses' station. The woman in charge was a friend, Sheila Kenner.

"I got word from base security to be on our toes. The German public is in an uproar about Hassani being in our hospital. They want us to turn him over to their government to deal with him."

"I saw some of the TV footage. Is security worried the crowd will storm the gates and hospital to get their man?" Erin asked. "I mean, there really aren't any gates to hold them back. Just a few security guards, who'd probably let them through if they got mean."

"Cyber intel indicates increased activity with the Taliban and Al-Qaeda elements active in the area." Sheila brought up an email on her computer screen and pointed to the announcement. "Nothing substantive, but they warned us to be aware."

On foreign soil, receiving threat warnings from the

base security staff wasn't unusual. Erin nodded. "Will do."

At seven the following morning, she went through shift change with the nurse coming on duty. Once she'd handed over her responsibilities, Erin hurried to the ward where Caesar was recovering.

His bed was empty and freshly made with clean sheets, ready for the next patient.

Her heart skipped several beats.

"If you're looking for the SEAL, he's in the hospital cafeteria."

Erin spun to face a nurse wearing green scrubs with a nametag that read Reynolds. "The cafeteria?"

The young woman smiled. "I had a hard time convincing him this morning was too soon to make the trek, but the man was stubborn. As soon as he heard the doc's okay, he was on his feet before the doc left the floor. And he's been up five times since. At this rate, he'll return to duty in days." The nurse tilted her head. "You're one of the CCATT nurses who brought him in, aren't you?"

"Yes, I am." Erin didn't want to be rude, but she also didn't want to hang around and talk to the chatty nurse. But she couldn't come up with an excuse to leave.

Reynolds grinned. "He's quite the charmer. I wonder if he's married."

"I wouldn't know."

"He doesn't wear a ring, but then I wouldn't expect a SEAL to wear one." She patted the sheets. "I've always been a sucker for a man with tattoos. He was telling me about the different ones and the meaning behind them. I especially like that he has the SEAL Trident on his shoulder. It's impressive."

Her patience dissolving, Erin stepped aside. "If you'll excuse me, I have some business to attend to." She didn't, unless you counted having coffee with a SEAL who didn't mind telling stories about the tattoos on his body to every strange woman he encountered. Caesar was a natural flirt, which only went to prove her fears about the man.

He was playing with her and he'd forget her as soon as she left his sight. Hadn't he with Reynolds? Anger built as she marched across the hospital to the cafeteria.

She found him with a cup of coffee gripped between two big hands, sitting across the table from a pretty corporal in Army camouflage, her hair pulled back in a neat knot at her nape, her lips parted in a smile.

That did it. She obeyed her first inclination to turn and leave the cafeteria, find the next transport back to Bagram and forget about the SEAL who'd made her heart beat faster and her blood run hot.

In the middle of turning, she heard his deep sexy voice call out, "Lt. McGee!"

For a moment, she debated walking out without acknowledging him, but then she was almost certain he'd come running after her to the best of his ability. The nurse in her didn't want him to reinjure himself so soon, though the jealous woman wanted to tell him to go to hell.

"I have to get back to work." The corporal stood, tucked an imaginary hair behind her ear, her cheeks flushed pink. "Will you be around much longer?"

"Not if I can help it," he said, his gaze on Erin. "I'd like to return to my duty assignment and my team."

"Well, thanks again for taking the time to talk to me about my boyfriend. I'm sure you're right and he's just worried about me."

"You take care of yourself, Abby. Everything will work out."

"Thanks." She stepped past Erin, her eyes growing wide, her body stiffening when she noticed the rank on her uniform. "Excuse me, ma'am."

Erin nodded without saying a word.

"Lt. McGee." Caesar pushed to his feet, wincing. He wore the hospital gown and a hospital-issued robe and still managed to look hot. Apparently, he'd showered, but he had opted not to shave, and his hair was on the shaggy side, like most SEALs on deployment. "I saved a place for you." He held out a chair.

Erin hesitated when she should have kept walking right out of the man's life.

"You promised coffee if I was up on my own two feet." He grinned and held out his muscular arms. "I'm on my own two feet. I even made it down here without a wheelchair or assistance from the nurses."

"I can imagine you had plenty of volunteers," she snapped.

His brows furrowed. "Have I done something wrong?"

Erin glanced around at the others in the cafeteria. Some faces had turned their way. Rather than become a spectacle in front of the military and civilian personnel there for breakfast and their coffee, she closed the distance between her and Caesar. But she didn't take the seat. "I'm not staying."

"Why?"

"Why should I? I'm sure you have plenty of women standing in line to sit and chat with you." She swallowed hard. "And I have to get some sleep. I'm on duty again tonight."

He captured her hand and refused to let go. "I don't care about any of the other women. I only want to have coffee with you."

"You were doing just fine with your little friend a moment ago." God, she hated how waspish her voice sounded. But, damn it, she couldn't contain her anger.

His frown deepened and he glanced around in confusion, then his brows lifted and he smiled. "You mean Abby?" He chuckled. "She's a nice kid, all worried about her boyfriend back home. We ran into each other in the checkout line. The poor girl was almost in tears."

"There's Abby and then there's Reynolds, your nurse."

"Jennifer?"

"See?" She jerked at his grasp but couldn't retrieve her hand. "You know her first name. And she says you're quite the charmer."

"Me?" His frown returned. "You're not jealous of Jennifer and Abby, are you?"

"Of course, I'm not jealous." Erin realized her voice had increased in volume. Another glance around at the faces turned her direction made her drop into the proffered seat.

Caesar eased into the one beside her. "Then why mention them? They're nice women, but they don't mean anything to me. You're the only woman I'm interested in."

"For now." Erin turned her head and stared at the line of customers at the cash register. In her peripheral vision, she could see Caesar studying her, his brown gaze soft and worried.

After a while, he leaned closer. "I won't be interested in anyone else."

"It doesn't matter. I came to tell you we can't see each other. I could lose my commission, and anything between us will never last anyway."

His lips drew into a thin line. "Why couldn't it?"

"You're a SEAL. I'm in the Air Force. You're enlisted, I'm an officer. Do I have to spell it out...again?"

He shook his head. "You're looking at it all wrong. You see all the reasons we can't be together."

"What other way is there?" She sighed, her shoulders slumping, exhaustion claiming her.

His lips lifted in a tender smile. "I see all the reasons why we should."

Though the smile made her knees and her resolve weaken, she refused to let him see it. Pushing back her shoulders, she gave him a pointed stare. "Tell me one."

"We like the same kind of music."

Erin frowned. "How do you know? We haven't even dated."

"I made it my business to find out." His chest swelled. "You like soft rock, but when you work out, you prefer something a little more hard core."

He's right. "Lucky guess."

"Maybe. The point is that I like soft rock and I like to work out to something with a faster pace. Like you." He waved a hand between them. "When you go dancing, you prefer country western because you like to two-step." He flattened a palm on his chest. "I like to dance, and if you like to two-step, I bet you'll like salsa as well. I can teach you to salsa, if you don't already know how."

Erin's chest tightened. She'd met Matthew at the Ramstein Air Force Base Officer's Club. He'd danced with her, but never really got the rhythm of the music. Having resigned herself to a relationship with little dancing, she had given up on finding a man who could dance, telling herself the activity wasn't a deal-breaker. That Caesar enjoyed dancing and wanted to teach her to salsa made the decision to walk away just a little bit harder.

With another heavy sigh, she noted, "You're missing the point. I'm not in the market for a relationship."

"You weren't until you met me." He touched his thumb to his chest and gave her a sexy smile.

Butterflies fluttered in her belly and she swayed toward him and his all-too-charming smile. "You're far too sure of yourself. Some people would call that conceit."

"I call it confidence." He squeezed her hand. "I see a woman who has been burned by a man who couldn't keep his fly zipped, and is afraid to trust a man because that betrayal hurt." He wove his fingers with hers. "I'm not that man."

"You're a SEAL." Her chest tightened. "To be a SEAL, you have to be something of an adrenaline junky."

He nodded. "I am, a little."

"Adrenaline junkies can't help themselves. They get

bored easily. One woman would never satisfy an adrenaline junky."

His brows rose up into the dark hair falling over his forehead. "Is that what the dumbass told you?"

How did he guess? Erin glanced away. "Maybe." Matthew had told her exactly that, as an excuse for fooling around with another woman while dating her. As if his behavior was an uncontrollable birth defect she shouldn't hold against him. And, yes, his betrayal had stung and still made her mad.

"Trust me when I say, I don't treat women as conquests. I don't need that kind of adrenaline high. And I didn't join the SEALs because I wanted on the adrenaline roller coaster." He settled back in the chair. "I wanted to be part of something elite, a team that trained together and pulled as one. There are no individuals on my SEAL team. We fight as a team and we succeed as a team. That's what drew me to apply." His grip tightened.

"Yeah, but that doesn't resolve the fact that you're constantly deployed, and so am I."

"I learned something long before I became a SEAL, and everything I've done since then has reinforced it. Where there is a will, you find a way. I'm willing. The question is, are you?"

"I can't." She stared down at his hand. "A relationship goes against the rules, and I barely know you."

She chocked back a laugh. "Nurse Reynolds knows more about you than I do."

"Then at least give yourself a chance to get to know me." He cupped her hand in both of his. "Even though my heritage is Hispanic, I like Italian food the best. My favorite color is green, like your eyes, because it reminds me of spring. I have two brothers and two sisters and they are all younger. My brothers are in the Marine Corps. One of my sisters is studying to be a nurse like you, and my youngest sister is still in high school." One corner of his mouth quirked upward. "She worships me, so I try very hard to set a good example."

Erin's heart squeezed in her chest. All those things she didn't know about him made him all the more appealing. "You're making it hard for me to say no."

"Good. That's what I was aiming for." He stared into her eyes. "Your parents are still alive and live in Virginia. Your father is retired Army and he probably inspired you to join the military. Am I right?"

Her throat tightened. He'd gone to a lot of trouble to learn things about her. She nodded. "He did. Though he wasn't thrilled. However, he was happy I chose to go into the Air Force instead of the Army."

"You had one brother, who joined the Army when you were in nursing school."

Throat suddenly dry, Erin tightened her hand

around his. Like Caesar's little sister, Erin had worshipped her older brother.

"Unfortunately, he died in an IED explosion." Caesar's voice lowered to a gentle whisper. "I'm sorry. You must have loved him very much."

Tears welled in her eyes, but she refused to let them fall. "It's been three years."

"You never get over losing a loved one."

She couldn't stop herself from asking, "What about your parents?"

"Both are still alive." He nodded. "My mother and father didn't graduate from high school until they were in their forties and took the GED. They are second-generation Americans, and they refused to let even one of us slack off in school. They were determined we would have a better life than they'd had."

"Sounds like they were successful."

"The jury's still out. Celina has to get through school, yet." He laughed. "I'll kick her butt if she even thinks about dropping out. She's a junior. One more year and all my parent's children will have graduated high school."

"You are close to your family?"

Grinning, he nodded. "I love them very much. I learned from watching my parents that love can last a very long time."

Erin pulled her fingers from his grasp and stood, agitation stiffening her muscles. "I thought love was supposed to last as well. And though my parents both live in Virginia, they divorced when I was sixteen." She turned and walked a few steps away, before facing him again. "The truth is that whatever exists between you and me isn't meant to be."

"Ah, see?" Caesar's eyes widened and the smile on his face broadened. "You admit there is something between us."

Couldn't he see? Their situation was hopeless. "No, there can't be."

His smile didn't slip, his eyes warming. "I have more convincing to do."

She held up her hands. "Please, there's nothing to prove. Just let it go."

"I can't." He stood, his jaw tightening with the effort. "You see, I'm a hopeless romantic. I believe in love, and Lt. McGee, I'm falling hopelessly in love with you."

His words hit her square in the chest, making her heart squeeze hard enough to hurt. "Well, then fall out of love, because after my shift tonight, I'm headed back to the sandbox."

"Then I'm going, too."

"Not until you're fully recovered."

He straightened and squared his shoulders. "I'm just as good as new."

"You're not." She backed away.

"Erin, wait." When he followed, his face creased in pain.

"Like I said. The doc won't release you to duty until you're fully recovered. That could take weeks."

"Days," he argued, his lips tightening. "I'll be back in under a week."

"And in theater, nothing can happen. Nothing will." Though her heart was pulling for her to stay and have that damned cup of coffee, she knew cutting it off now was the best decision for both of them. "Don't prolong this. I won't change my mind."

"If you won't change your mind..." he tipped his head and braced his fingertips on the tabletop, "very well." Then he let her go.

As she walked away, she could hear him whisper beneath his breath.

His words sounded something like, "I will have to change your mind for you."

Caesar's backside ached by the time he made it back to his bed.

"You shouldn't push it so much." Nurse Reynolds read him the riot act. "You don't want to inflame the wound area or you could cause damage to your spinal cord. Personally, I'd rather see you walking out of here than strapped in a wheelchair."

"Yes, ma'am." He eased into the bed, surprised at how tired he was after such a short walk. More than anything, the emotions of his conversation with Erin had drained him. How could he convince the pretty lieutenant he was sincere, when he was lying flat on his back in a hospital bed?

He had until she went on duty that night to do something. But for the next couple hours, he'd conserve his strength.

The nurse took his pulse and blood pressure.

Caesar lay back, watching her movements. "Lieutenant Reynolds?"

"Yes, Caesar."

"Why are women so difficult to understand?"

She laughed. "What's to understand? All we want is to be loved." Her brows rose. "Speaking of which...are you married, engaged, or otherwise spoken for?"

As he remembered the sight of Erin walking away, he twisted his lips. "No, but I hope to be."

"Got anyone in mind, or can I take a shot?"

Her open face and smile were compelling, but she wasn't Erin. "I'm flattered, but I have my heart set on someone else."

"She wouldn't happen to have auburn hair and green eyes, would she?"

He shot a glance at the perky Nurse Reynolds. "She might."

"You have your work cut out."

"You know her?"

"I've heard about the LT. She was burned by a pilot who cheated on her."

Caesar nodded. "So, she doesn't trust men."

"Hard to trust your heart, when it's been broken." Nurse Reynolds laid a hand on his arm. "If you really love her, and you're not just challenged because she turned you down, then you have to keep trying."

"That's the second time someone has referred to what I'm feeling as challenged. I like to think I'm more of a man than that."

"Some men get off on wooing women who turn them down. And once they win them, they're done. Bored." With a frown, she wiped her hands together and flung them in the air. "On to the next woman."

Caesar snorted. "Bastards. A woman is supposed to be loved and cherished, not used up and thrown out."

Jennifer squeezed his arm. "If you lose out with your girl, will you remember me? I'm looking for just such a man as you."

After the nurse left, Caesar turned over her words in his mind. No wonder Erin was hesitant to commit to a relationship. He didn't blame her. But she'd been there the night they'd gone on their mission. She'd initiated that kiss after making love to him. She might not want to admit it, but there was something there.

No matter how hard Erin pushed back, Caesar refused to give up. He'd find a way to convince her he wasn't a jerk like the pilot.

Finding the right way to prove it would be his test.

6

————

Erin returned to the room she'd been assigned at base lodging, stripped out of her uniform and stepped into the shower. Over and over, her confrontation with Caesar replayed through her mind.

The officer in her verified she'd done the right thing. The woman who'd been lied to and cheated on cautioned her about not getting involved. But the innocent young woman who still held onto those silly childhood dreams of happily ever after wanted the future to be with Caesar. And the lusty, grown woman, who'd tasted what had been the best sex of her life, ached to return to his bedside, crawl in and make love with the sexy SEAL.

After squirting a handful of shampoo into her palm, she scrubbed her hair. Then she went to work on her body, hoping to wash away the residual tingling from where his hand had touched her. Suds slipped over her shoulders and across her breasts, warm smooth and making her nerves stretch for the release she needed.

Erin rinsed the soap from her eyes and watched as the bubbles dripped off the tips of her budded nipples. Some slipped over her torso and downward to catch on the little tuft of curls over her mons.

With a groan, she followed the trail with her fingers, parting the folds to find that little nubbin of flesh in the middle. If Caesar were in the shower with her, his big, rough fingers would stroke her there. Perhaps he'd go down on her and slip his tongue inside her body.

Flicking herself, she moaned. How much better would the sensation be if she were with the man instead of pleasuring herself? She flicked herself again, warm water sliding down between her legs, heating her inner thighs.

He'd dip his tongue into her and taste her juices. Her finger followed the path of her memory, slipping into her channel, slick with her cream, and back out to tease the tightly packed bundle of nerves, swelled with need and aching for fulfillment. Swirling her finger around and around, she felt tension build and swell until her body stiffened and she threw back her head.

Warm water pelted her face as she came to her own

touch, dreaming of a particular SEAL's hands and mouth on her body.

Shaking with her release and yet still dissatisfied, Erin realized what could have made her orgasm more complete. Being held in strong arms, the SEAL's thick, hard erection sliding inside her, filling her like no cold, lonely vibrator could. Erin turned the shower setting to cold, dowsed her skin and raging body with icy water to chill her desire.

What good was dreaming about such things? The man resided in a hospital, recuperating from a spinal injury. Making love wasn't an option.

Unless she was on top.

The thought slipped into her mind and she banished it immediately. That was ridiculous. She couldn't go to a patient's bed, climb into it and make love to him in the hospital. That would go against all the rules and might put the patient at risk of reinjuring him.

Stop it! Stop thinking about Caesar.

Erin buried her face in a towel and rubbed at her skin. No amount of scrubbing or chastising herself would wipe the man from her mind. Nothing would, now that she'd made love to him. The best she could do was hit the road and run him out of her system.

She dug into her backpack, found a PT shirt, shorts and her tennis shoes. In minutes, she was outside of the lodging and running in the damp, cool German air.

ELLE JAMES

Caesar followed, never far from her mind. She ran faster. Every breath she took included an image of Caesar smiling at her with the confidence of a charmer. His entire countenance was one of a man who'd already won the battle and waited to claim his prize.

Damn the man. Erin ran faster.

She found herself on the road leading toward the front gate. A huge crowd gathered outside, shouting and chanting, holding up signs written mostly in German, some in English.

Death to a Murderer!

Unwilling to get too close to the angry mob, Erin turned and ran the opposite direction. The angry tone of the shouting and chanting drove her back to the safety of the hospital walls.

By the time she entered, she was hungry and thirsty. She risked hitting the cafeteria, half-afraid, half-excited about the possibility that Caesar would still be there.

A sigh of relief mixed with disappointment. His was not one of the faces in the crowd. She quickly drank a glass of juice, forced herself to eat a bowl of oatmeal and then went in search of information about the next flight to Bagram. She needed to get back to work and away from temptation.

After making the arrangements to be on a flight out

that left the next afternoon, she headed back to her room. The night on duty, a run that had taken the steam out of her, and the added stress of her forbidden desire for one hot Navy SEAL all wore on her energy level. She'd sleep it off and when she woke, she'd have a fresh perspective and perhaps she'd get her head on straight.

A quick shower, sans the masturbation this time, a brisk towel across her skin and Erin was ready for bed. She slipped a T-shirt over her head and crawled between the sheets, pulling them up to her chin in the cool air.

Yeah, warm arms would feel great about now.

No. She had to stop thinking that way. She didn't need a man in her life. She was an independent woman who could take care of herself and her own needs.

As she slipped into sleep, she was betrayed by her dreams, settling her in the arms of a tattooed, Navy SEAL with brown-black hair and eyes so dark they appeared to be mirrors of his soul.

"Caesar, why are you here?" she asked the SEAL.

He kissed her, his lips trailing across her chin and down the length of her throat. "Because you asked me to come."

"But it's wrong." As wrong as it was, she didn't push him away. The sheet fell away and she was naked before him.

"How could it be wrong?" He teased a turgid nipple with the tip of his tongue. "You're in a dream."

A single tear slipped down her cheek and she whispered, "Because, I want it to be a reality."

A knock at her door broke the mood. Caesar disappeared into a fog.

Another knock forced Erin awake and she sat up, her hand going to the breast Caesar had flicked with his tongue.

"Lt. McGee?" a voice called out.

Erin threw aside the comforter and climbed out of bed, her brain still fogged with her dream. Grabbing a pair of shorts, she slipped them on as another knock sounded.

When she opened the door, she was greeted by a dozen bright red roses. The bouquet shifted and the delivery girl smiled. "These are for you."

Erin accepted the bouquet and closed the door. Who knew she was in Landstuhl? She ripped into the envelope accompanying the flowers.

You are more beautiful than a dozen red roses. CS

Erin shook her head. The scent of the roses filled the small room, their brilliant red seeming to be the only color in the otherwise colorless decor. She buried her nose in their soft petals and inhaled. Matt had never bought her roses, or flowers of any kind. He'd taken her out to dinner, but they'd always ended up in bed. After a while, the sex felt more like payment for the meal. Why had she put up with him for so long? A real man who cared would want to be with her for more than the sex.

A brief glance at the clock on the nightstand, and the rumbling in her belly, confirmed she'd slept for more than six hours. Plenty of sleep to gird her stamina for a long night shift. Now all she needed was fuel to see her through. After her shift ended, she'd be on a plane to Afghanistan, leaving Caesar behind.

Saddened at the thought, she dressed quickly in her flight suit, tucked her hair into a tight bun and dragged on her boots. Every movement was performed by rote memory. She'd dressed this way so often she could do it in the dark, and did, half the time. The difference being the way she felt as her clothes skimmed across her skin, reminding her of how Caesar's hands had caressed her.

Another glance at the clock. If she hurried, she could go by his room under the pretext of checking on her patient. Her pulse kicked up and she hurriedly finished tying her boots. As she stepped out of the building, she spotted the bus pulling up to the curb and she hopped on board. In minutes, she was at the entrance of the hospital.

Her heart thumping against her ribs, she forced herself to walk a sedate pace to the ward where Caesar was recuperating. Would stealing a kiss be possible? Of course, only to thank him for the flowers. Her blood burned through her veins as she passed storage room doors, and waiting rooms, her mind scoping for a quiet place where they could be alone.

Stop fooling yourself.

This hospital was perhaps the busiest of all with wounded soldiers and their families filling twenty-four/seven.

As she approached the door to his room, she drew in a deep breath, smoothed her clammy hands over her flight suit and entered.

The bed was empty. Once again, the sheets were neatly folded and the bed made as if for the next patient.

"If you're looking for tall, dark and hunky, he's in the cafeteria, hoping to see you there."

Fighting back a gasp, Erin spun to face Lt. Reynolds. "Uh, I was just coming to check on him. I like to know that the patients I help transport are doing better."

"Oh, he's doing fine, and you don't have to pretend with me." Lt Reynolds shook her head. "If he didn't have it bad for you, I'd have thrown my hat in the ring. That man's worth every risk."

Erin couldn't agree with the woman more, but she wouldn't in public. "Well, thank you. Would you please tell him I stopped by?"

"Tell him yourself when you see him in the cafeteria." The lieutenant winked. "Look, rules were meant to be broken. I'd sure break a few to be with Caesar."

"Thanks." Too wound up with the need to see him before she went on duty, Erin didn't bother to lie to the younger nurse. Obviously, her face told the story. She was in danger of falling for the man. Hell, she was already in too deep.

Erin made the long trek to the dining room, searching for his face down the long hallways, hoping to catch him if he was on his way back. By the time she reached the cafeteria, she'd stared at every face and come up short one SEAL.

Standing at the entrance to the large cafeteria, she scanned the sea of faces. Being dinnertime, the room was full and noisy with everyone talking at once. After several minutes, she realized his face wasn't among those present.

Heart heavy, she turned to the clock on the wall. She didn't have time to go back to his room. She barely had time to wolf down a bagel and a cup of coffee, scalding her tongue in the process. Five minutes later, with a burned tongue and a heart filled with disappointment, she headed for the ICU for shift change.

"You have Hassani again," the departing nurse briefed her as she handed over the chart. "We pulled his intubation tube this morning but he's still on oxygen. I just checked his IVs and drainage tubes. He should be good to go for a couple hours."

After they both went over the patient's chart and blood work, the nurse left and Erin was on her own to care for their prisoner.

Erin met the shift supervisor at the desk. "Hi, Sheila, anything new?"

Sheila looked up from her computer screen. "So far so good."

"The riots calm any?"

"From what I understand, the German polizei cracked down on the rioters and sent them packing earlier this evening."

"That's good news." Again, Erin checked her charts and made notes on fluid levels, pulse and blood pressure. "I bet you'll be glad when they move this guy stateside."

"You know it. I don't like feeling like we're under the gun, so to speak."

"Imagine what our soldiers have to deal with in theater. This is nothing compared."

"I know. Experiencing this brings it home to me and working on a patient who has caused so much death and destruction to our own troops becomes much more difficult."

"Ditto." Erin glanced toward the windowed room where Hassani lay recuperating after a life-saving operation. Her grip on the chart tightened. He'd been afforded care he would never have given to any of his prisoners. "Let's hope he can shed light on where the four soldiers are."

"If there's even a chance of getting that information, the effort will have been worth it. I know if my son were one of those U.S. soldiers being held, I'd do anything to find him." Sheila's gaze narrowed before she continued, "Even give medical care to the enemy."

Erin's lips twisted in a wry grin. "We'd do it anyway. It's the nature of our business."

Sheila smiled. "Right. But sometimes doing that is hard."

A couple hours later, Erin stopped at the nurses' counter and stretched. "I could use a bathroom break. Can you cover for me for just a few minutes?"

"Go. I'll keep track of your patient."

"Thanks."

Erin hurried to the bathroom and locked the door behind her. At one in the morning, they were halfway through the shift and she was already tired. Part of her problem was that she was thinking too much about a certain sexy SEAL, instead of what she needed to do to get through the night. Every time she turned around, she became aware of something that reminded her of Caesar. Just seeing Hassani reminded her of what she'd learned. Caesar had carried the man out of the village, thus saving his life.

She wished she could have seen him before she'd reported for duty. The scent of roses lingered in her memory and she wanted to thank him. No matter how many times he heard how they couldn't be together, the man didn't give up. If nothing else, he was persistent. Did that mean he really cared about her?

Her breath caught and held.

Maybe.

She breathed out.

He knew all the right things to say. If he wasn't sincere, he was well practiced in what a woman wanted to hear. From talking about sunsets, to dancing and roses, he was well on his way to stealing her heart.

Erin used the facilities and washed her hands, staring at her image in the mirror. The shadows beneath her eyes were more pronounced and she looked more haggard than usual. Turning on the cool water, she splashed a handful over her face. For a moment, she thought she heard something over the sound of the water running. She shut off the faucet and listened. Footsteps sounded outside the door followed by muffled shouts.

"Stop! You can't go in there."

That was Sheila's voice shouting. Erin's heart skipped several beats and raced on as she pressed her ear to the door.

Someone spoke in what sounded like Pashto, the language of the Taliban and Al-Qaeda. Her pulse hammered so hard against her eardrums she could barely hear.

The distinctive noise of metal gears and bolts being

shot home reached her through the heavy door. From the sound of the action, the ICU was being overrun by someone. Probably related to the Taliban. Erin's first instinct was to reach for the doorknob, yank it open and demand that they get the hell out. But reason kicked in and she didn't turn the knob. If she alerted them to her location, what would they do?

"Don't do that. He'll die," Sheila called out, her voice muffled, strained. "Let go of me, you baboon!" A loud clapping sound was followed by a whomp.

Her body tensed. Had they hurt Sheila?

Unable to remain still a moment longer, Erin eased around the doorknob and eased the door open enough to peer out.

She pressed her hand over her mouth to smother a gasp. Six men dressed in black and carrying weapons stood in the ICU. Four were in the room with Hassani, loading him on a litter, transferring his IVs to the hooks attached to the mobile cart.

From where she stood, Erin could see Sheila lying on the floor, a pool of blood spreading across the clean tiles. Was she dead? Erin studied her body, hoping for the tell-tale sign of her lungs expanding. Her eyes blinked open, and she stared across the floor at Erin and gave her just the slightest shake of her head.

As soon as Hassani was unplugged from his monitors, alarms went off. The men near the nurses' station jumped and rounded to other side, pressing buttons frantically and then used the butts of their rifles to smash the equipment, ending the beeping.

With Hassani loaded, the men rushed toward the exit.

They would pass by the door Erin hid behind. She closed the door carefully, praying they hadn't noticed the movement.

Footsteps hurried past, the squeak of the wheels on the litter indicating they'd moved by.

Erin inched the door open again. The knob was yanked out of her hand and a man with a black mask and turban grabbed her arm, dragged her out of the bathroom and shoved a knife against her throat.

Caesar spent the day in and out of his hospital bed. More out than in. Knowing Erin would be sleeping away the day, he couldn't bring himself to disturb her any earlier than he had to. He did the next best thing. He walked to the gift shop in the hospital, had the attendant help him find Erin's quarters and then ordered flowers to be delivered in the afternoon, after she'd had enough time to sleep.

Though she still resisted any claim to a relationship with him, Caesar knew it was only a matter of time before she caved. After making love with her behind the supply building, he refused to give up on being with her. She wouldn't have responded so wantonly if she didn't feel something for him.

He understood her hesitation. The fraternization

rule was a huge obstacle to overcome, but others had done so. The Air Force couldn't afford to lose a highly qualified CCATT nurse. As much training as he'd undergone as a SEAL, he knew the Navy wouldn't part with him because he had fallen in love with an officer in an entirely different branch of service. His best bet would be to woo her while they were still in Germany, away from the stricter fraternization rules of theater deployment. Which didn't give him much time. If the determination in her face at their last meeting was anything to go by, she'd already arranged her flight back to Afghanistan.

He had to see her. While he'd been at the gift shop, he'd purchased a Landstuhl T-shirt, a pair of sweatpants and shower shoes. The doctor had been by around noon to check out his incisions and stitches, claiming he would soon be fit for release. Caesar pretended he was in more pain than he was to get the doc to agree to hold him one day longer.

As the hour the flowers were supposed to be delivered came and went, Caesar dressed in the newly purchased clothes, careful not to disturb his bandages and stitches. He fully expected to fly back to Afghanistan within a couple days. His injuries had been nothing compared to others here at the hospital.

Afraid he'd miss her, Caesar left his room and headed for the cafeteria. A quick glance around was enough to know Erin hadn't arrived. With less than an hour before she reported to duty, she should have been inside eating dinner.

Unless she'd stopped by his room on the way. In which case, he might have missed her. Caesar hurried back to his room, running into Lt. Reynolds in the hallway.

"If you're looking for the pretty red-haired nurse, she came and left. She told me to thank you for the flowers. I let her know you'd gone to the cafeteria."

"I didn't see her there."

"You must have missed her."

"Damn." Regret tugged at his achy body. "She goes on duty in fifteen minutes." He glanced around. "Which way is ICU?"

"Building 3711, third floor." The lieutenant grabbed his arm before he could leave. "Won't do you any good. They aren't letting any nonessential personnel inside while Hassani is there. I heard they have MPs guarding the doors. Not even family members can go in."

"Seriously?" His heart sank into his shower shoes. His chances of seeing Erin narrowing, Caesar held onto the thought that at the very least, he'd catch Erin coming off her shift in the morning.

"You might as well get some rest. Do you want me to give you something to ease your non-existent pain?" Reynolds asked. "I intend to have the doc kick your ass out of here and make room for patients who actually need medical attention."

Just what I need to hear. He winked. "You'd miss me if you did that."

"Careful, froggy. Your girlfriend might get jealous and think you're flirting. Not that I mind, but she seemed pretty stuck on you and you've made yourself clear."

Whoa, what is this? He focused his gaze on the informative nurse. "You think she's stuck on me?"

"She'd be stupid if she wasn't."

A shoulder lifted in a shrug, but hope had his pulse racing. "She's a tough nut to crack."

"Yeah, but that kind is all soft and gooey on the inside when you do." Lt. Reynolds tilted her head. "Got any more like you where you come from? I could use a hero to save me from slitting my wrists out of sheer boredom."

"Plenty more where I came from. Care to make a trip out to the sandbox?"

"In a heartbeat." She sighed. "I keep asking, but my commander says they need me on site."

"You're doing a great service to the troops who have to come through here."

"I know. It's a great job and the patients are amazing. Don't mind my drool as I go back to work." She nodded toward his room. "And you should head to bed. You don't want to reinjure yourself."

With a sigh, he followed her back to his room.

Lt. Reynolds checked his pulse and blood pressure

and gave him his vitamin and pain medication. "Go on, take it. You told the doc you were still hurting. The pill will also help you sleep so that you're rested when you go looking for your red-head in the morning."

"Fine." He downed the pills, washing them away with the cup of water on the stand next to his bed. Since he couldn't get into ICU to see Erin, he might as well sleep away the night. Tomorrow, he'd check on flights back to Bagram. If there was one, he was afraid Erin would have booked a seat. He wanted to be on it, as well, his thoughts going to his team. He hoped they were all right without him. Kicking backward with his arms behind his head, he counted the minutes until he'd see Erin again.

Within half an hour, he was snoring.

Caesar ran up a hill, the body on his back weighing him down, making his steps slower and slower, like when he'd slogged through knee-deep mud. The helicopter engines roared ahead, the blades turning faster and faster. He had to get there before they took off.

Sting Ray, carrying a man on his back, sprinted past him, grinning like an idiot, reaching the helo in time to dump his load and climb aboard. No matter how hard he ran, Caesar got no closer. The helicopter hovered an inch off the ground, rising slowly.

No! You can't leave without me.

Caesar stumbled and fell, his legs refusing to hold his weight. He tried to stand, but when he looked down, he had no legs. Horror filled his gut. No. This isn't happening.

He left the body he'd been carrying on the ground and clawed his way toward the helicopter. As it lifted off, he grasped the skid. The helo rose off the ground, but his arms were too weak to hold on. He fell back to the surface with a hard thud that shook him awake.

Caesar jerked to a sitting position and stared around, heart pounding double time. The desert sand was gone. In its place were the clean white walls of a hospital room. Instead of hard ground beneath him, he lay on a soft mattress with clean sheets and blankets. Still wearing his sweats and T-shirt, he swung his legs over the side. A twinge of pain reminded him of the stitches in his back, buttocks and thighs. With more care, he slipped off the bed, thankful when his legs held his weight. The dream had been so vivid, he thought for sure his legs would give out.

Too wound up and disturbed by his nightmare, he left his room, determined to walk off the residual adrenaline.

At this hour, the hallways were empty of visitors and patients, only nurses and the occasional doctor passed him.

One nurse stopped him and gripped his arm. "Shouldn't you be in bed?"

"Thank you, but I need to move."

She studied his face. "I can look at your chart and see if the doctor left instructions for sleep medication."

"No, thank you. I really just need to walk."

"Well, we don't like patients to wander around. If you should fall..."

"Fine. I'll go back to bed." He performed an about-face and walked back the way he'd come, ducking into a maintenance closet where disinfectants, mops and brooms were located. And spotted one slightly soiled hospital maintenance coverall.

Caesar slipped into the coverall, thankful the previous wearer was a large man. He had room to zip up the top, when most shirts and jackets didn't fit over his muscular frame. Acting the part, he pushed a mop and empty bucket out into the hallway and headed for building 3711.

Twice, a nurse stopped him to clean up a spill. He did so, thankful they didn't catch on that he was a patient and thus should be safely asleep in his bed. As he neared building 3711, he noted the number of people in the hallway had dwindled down to none.

Had they cleared all personnel to safeguard their prisoner?

Still pushing the mop bucket, Caesar proceeded quietly down the hallway, the silence eerie and unnerving. As he passed a room, he heard an agonized moan. He glanced at the ground where a dark smear led underneath the door.

Though he wanted to proceed to the ICU and find out what the hell was going on, he couldn't ignore the cry. Heart pounding, he pushed through a door and stared at a man in combat uniform wearing an MP armband. His face looked like hamburger meat, red, purple and raw, as if someone had bashed him several times with something heavy. Both his eyes were swollen nearly shut and blood ran freely from his nose. He'd been bound, gagged and dragged into the room.

With his nose smashed, the man couldn't get enough air and he struggled with each breath. Caesar yanked the gag out of his mouth and searched for something to break through his bindings. "What happened?" he asked.

"Ambushed," the MP croaked.

"Who?"

"Don't know. They wore masks and black turbans. Headed for ICU. Where's my partner, Rothe?" He coughed and spit out blood.

"You're the first person I came across. How many more MPs were there in the building?"

The man stared up at him, his eyes narrowing.

"Look, I'm one of the good guys. I'm Navy SEAL Caesar Sanchez."

The man's frown eased. "Two MP's on each floor of building 3711, and two at each entrance to the hospital."

Caesar tore at the knots binding the man's wrists

and ankles, afraid he was taking too long. If the attackers were headed for ICU...

Dear God. Erin.

As soon as he freed the MP, he stood, using the mop handle for support. "I'm headed to the ICU. Think you can get back down the hallway and sound a quiet alert?"

The young MP squinted through his swollen eyes. "I think so."

"Tell them to come in quietly. No major alarms. We don't want the terrorists randomly killing if they're spooked."

"Yes, sir."

Caesar helped the man to his feet and to the door. He peered out, verifying the hallway was clear. He pointed the man in the right direction. "Go."

Staggering, with his hand running along the wall, the MP hurried back the way Caesar had come.

Turning the opposite direction, Caesar sprinted toward the ICU. On the first floor now, he had to get to the third floor. Whatever faction had staged the attack could have left guards along the way.

Avoiding the elevator, Caesar found a stairwell. As he eased the door open, he nearly tripped over the body on the other side.

Wearing the same uniform as the other MP, he sported a name tag with Rothe written across it.

Fuck.

Pressing two fingers to the carotid artery in Rothe's neck, Caesar held his breath. After a moment, he felt the reassuring thump of a pulse. Though the guard was injured, he showed no signs of an open wound. Caesar searched him for a weapon. His holster was empty.

Caesar left him, slipped out of his shower shoes and moved silently up the stairs to the second floor, easing around each turn, checking for enemy guards. When he arrived at the third floor, he peered through the window in the door, looking in both directions.

Two men dressed in dark clothes, ski masks and black turbans held AK-47's and stood guard at the door to the ICU. They waited, weapons at the ready, facing the elevator.

Caesar eased away from the door, ran back down to the second floor, checked for signs of enemy and rushed to the elevator. He pushed the button, the doors opened and he stepped in, pressed the button for the third floor and stepped back into the hallway.

Running back to the stairwell, he ignored the pain in his backside and took the stairs two at a time to the top and then paused, wincing at the pain in his backside.

When the elevator dinged, the two men left their posts and hurried toward the door as it slid open, pointing their weapons at the elevator car.

Caesar eased open the stairwell door and slipped

through, closing it softly behind him. Moving with the stealth of a cat, he sneaked up behind the closest man, grabbed him from behind and shoved him hard into the other man, knocking them both into the door of the elevator. They landed half-in and half-out of the opening.

Surprise was on his side. While the two men struggled to untangle themselves, Caesar ripped the rifle from the hands of the nearest man, slammed the butt of the weapon into his head and swung it upward to clip the second man in the chin. Neither man had the opportunity to use their weapons. The elevator door attempted to close, but wouldn't with the two men blocking the track.

Not knowing how much time he had before others might investigate the disturbance, Caesar dragged the men into the elevator and, using the straps on their weapons and their own turbans, he bound their arms and legs, quickly and effectively. After confiscating their guns and knives, he hit the button for the first floor and jumped back before the doors closed. Hopefully, the MP had made contact with the base security forces and they'd soon be on their way as backup.

Noise from the other side of the ICU doors alerted him to imminent danger. Caesar slipped into a waiting room, holding the AK-47 against his chest and peered around the edge of the entrance.

The door swung open and a litter was pushed

through, the big wheels bumping against the door, jolting the patient and making the IV bags on either side of his body swing wildly.

If Caesar wasn't mistaken, the patient was Hassani and the men taking him away were either members of the local Taliban or men dressed to resemble the Taliban or Al-Qaeda. They turned in the other direction and headed for the elevator.

Two more men emerged from the ICU, dragging a female hostage dressed in a dull green flight suit, kicking and fighting to the best of her ability.

One of the attackers sank his fingers into dark red hair and yanked hard, tipping back her head to press a knife to her throat. "Shut up, or I kill you and go back to kill your friend."

Erin.

Jaw clamped shut, Caesar's heart sputtered and kicked into high gear. One man against six terrorists was bad enough. But terrorists holding a hostage made it exponentially worse. Especially when the hostage was Erin.

Erin's struggles ceased. "I'll go with you. Just leave the other woman alone."

The man with the knife snorted and pushed her forward, still holding the knife to her neck, his arm clamped around both of hers.

The lead man spoke to the others in Pashto.

With his rough understanding of the language,

Caesar gathered they wondered what had happened to their guards.

The men glanced around and called out.

Caesar eased back behind the doorway, swinging his weapon over his shoulder.

A voice that sounded like the man who'd threatened Erin gave orders to search the rooms and find their men.

Footsteps pounded against the polished flooring, headed his way.

Forcing a calm breath, Caesar flattened himself against the wall just inside the waiting room.

One of the men in black stepped through the door, his gun resting in his crooked elbow.

When he'd gotten all the way inside and out of view of the others, Caesar jumped him, wrapped his arm around his neck and slit his throat.

Their struggle drew the attention of the others, and a second man entered the room, his gun in the lead. One glance at the man on the floor and he whipped around, firing his weapon.

Caesar dove, rolled behind some seats and fired back at the man, hitting him square in the chest.

The attacker jerked backward and fell out into the hallway.

Through the doorway poked the barrel of an AK-47.

"Throw down your gun or I kill the woman," the demand came in stilted English.

"Turn her loose and I might consider it," he responded through gritted teeth.

"Don't do it! They'll kill you!" Erin cried out.

The sound of a struggle and feminine grunts reached Caesar. Blocking out the cries, he had to make a plan. He'd counted six men, two of which were now dead. One of the four remaining held Erin hostage.

The ping of an arriving elevator rang out, followed by the swoosh of doors opening.

The man in charge gave an order that sounded like Kill him.

Then the squeak of wheels, more female grunts and pounding against the walls of what sounded like the inside of the elevator and the whisper of sliding doors closing.

Even before the swish of the elevator doors had finished, the barrel of an AK-47 poked around the doorframe of the waiting room. Caesar remained low, edged around an end table and aimed his weapon at the knees of the man who entered.

He fired off several rounds.

The man went down and another dropped down behind the first, levering him upward to use as a human shield.

Caesar tucked his weapon close to his chest and rolled behind a vinyl chair. The shooter fired, the bullets thumping into the back of the furniture, a few hitting the wall over Caesar's head.

He didn't have time to fool with the man. The terrorists were getting away with Hassani and would use Erin as their hostage to demand whatever they wanted. And if he didn't beat them to the first floor, he feared the security forces might shoot first, not realizing Erin was with them.

If he wanted to get to Erin, he had to eliminate the current threat. On the count of three. One...two... Caesar leaped from his position and dove to the left behind another couch, firing off a burst of bullets at the man lying behind the one he'd already felled.

A cry alerted him to the fact he'd hit the guy. How badly was yet to be determined. He tossed a People magazine to the right, and rolled to the left as bullets tore through the fluttering pages.

While the man aimed at the magazine, Caesar rose, aimed and pulled the trigger, hitting the man in the head. The room went silent except for the groans of the man whose knees he'd shot out and who now lay trapped beneath the deadweight of his comrade.

Caesar grabbed their weapons, removed the bullets, bolt and magazines, then slung them to the far corner of the room.

The live terrorist spit on him and cursed him in Pashto, dark eyes glaring.

Caesar ignored him, yanking the clothing off his

Taliban buddy. He dressed quickly in the dark pants and shirt and covered his head in the ski mask. He used the turban to bind the injured man and gag him. With little time to spare, he slung an AK-47 over his shoulder, tucked the spare magazines in his pocket and ran past the elevator, glancing upward. The light in the display window showed a glowing number two. Why would they have stopped at the second floor? To leave they'd have to go out on the first floor. Unless they were hunkering down and preparing to negotiate their release.

Caesar raced for the stairs and ran down to the second floor. An echoing clang indicated the door being opened on the first floor. Dressed as one of the terrorists, he couldn't afford to wait around for the MPs to find him in the stairwell. They'd shoot first and sift through bodies later. He glanced through the window of the stairwell door on the second floor. The hallway was empty. Pushing through the doorway, he eased it open and closed it softly behind him.

The click of a door shutting to his left alerted him to movement.

A woman screamed and was immediately quieted.

Following the noise, Caesar tiptoed silently on bare feet toward a corner in the hallway. He glanced up, aware of the mirror positioned high on the wall to allow people from both directions to see if someone was coming around the corner. Before he got close enough to be seen, he could make out a black blur. Probably a guard left to monitor the hallway.

Banking on his dark eyes and dark skin to aid his subterfuge, he stepped into view of the mirror and ran around the corner. Drawing on his elementary knowledge of Pashto, he said what he hoped was, "They come!" forcing urgency into his tone.

The man standing outside a door shouted and pointed his weapon at Caesar.

Caesar didn't slow, holding his weapon in front of him as if he wasn't afraid the Taliban man would shoot. When he got close enough, he stopped, and bent over, pretending to breathe hard from running, which wasn't far from the truth.

The man asked him something, but he didn't quite catch the wording. When he asked again, Caesar jerked upright, slammed the butt of his weapon into the man's face so hard, his nose broke. Grabbing his head, Caesar jerked his face down while bringing his knee up sharply.

The man fell unconscious against Caesar.

Catching him before he hit the floor, Caesar eased his body to the ground, dragging him down the hallway.

Behind the door where he stood, a cry rang out. Three terrorists, that he knew of, were holed up in the room with Erin. Wiping the blood from his hands onto the clothing of the man he'd dropped, he straightened and pushed the door open.

Relief filled him at the sight of Erin, standing beside one of her captors.

Inside, he was surrounded by two of the terrorists who immediately lowered their weapons.

Their leader pointed an AK-47 at Erin's temple.

She held a telephone handset to her ear, her finger hovering over the keypad.

"Tell them we want an ambulance out front now, or we blow up the entire building."

One of the two men with the leader spoke in short, urgent Pashto.

The leader glared and spoke back sharply.

The man nodded, a smirk curling the corners of his mouth through the ski mask.

Erin's lips were pulled into a tight line and her face was pale. Her left eye was swollen and turning purple, and her lower lip was cracked and bleeding.

Caesar fought the urge to start shooting and not stop until he'd killed all three of the terrorists for hurting Erin. But he couldn't. Not until he was certain Erin wouldn't be caught in the crossfire.

"Tell them!" The leader backhanded her.

P ain shot through Erin's head as it snapped around with the force of his hand. She raised her fingers to her cheek, hatred burning deep down. With shaky fingers, she punched in the emergency number and waited for someone to answer on the other end.

When she got the dispatcher, she spoke quickly. "This is Lt. Erin McGee. I'm being held at gunpoint inside the medical center, building 3711. Please connect me with someone with the authority to negotiate my release." She waited as dispatch connected the call.

"Lt. McGee, this is Colonel Allen, are you okay?"

"I'm okay for now, but I don't know for how long. Three men are trying to get our prisoner, Hassani Nurabi, to the airport. They're demanding an ambulance and safe passage for their group of four." She glanced around at the men. "They wanted me to tell you that they have explosive charges set at various points throughout the hospital, and they will detonate them one at a time, starting in five minutes if they don't get that ambulance."

"Tell them we'll have the ambulance waiting outside in less than three minutes," Colonel Allen said.

Erin let go of the breath she'd been holding. "I'll let them know."

"Lieutenant, stay on the line—

Her captor grabbed the telephone and slammed it onto the cradle.

She sat calmly and repeated what the colonel had told her. "They're bringing an ambulance around now."

"Good. You will come with us and care for our leader." The man glanced at Hassani, still unconscious on the litter. Erin had checked moments earlier for a pulse. He had one, but she didn't know how long it would last since they'd disconnected his oxygen. So far, he seemed to be breathing on his own.

Her captor's gaze shifted to the man who'd entered while Erin had been on the phone and he fired off a question at him in Pashto.

The man ducked his head and nodded, muttering something unintelligible.

Something about the way he stood, and the breadth of his shoulders made Erin look twice. For a moment, his gaze met hers. When recognition hit her, she gasped then pressed her lips tight.

Caesar.

The leader stood and asked another question. When the new man still didn't respond, the other two men leveled their weapons on him.

Heart hammering, Erin knew she had to do something to divert their attention. She flung herself at their leader and poked him in the eyes as hard as she could. The man screamed and staggered backward, arms windmilling and his knees catching against a chair. Seeing him off balanced, all she had to do was plant a hand in the middle of his chest to send him flying over the chair and crashing to the floor.

The terrorists swung from the slouching figure toward Erin.

Caesar plowed into them from the side, hitting the closest one, knocking him into the other. Both tripped over each other and landed flat on their backs, their weapons flying from their grasps.

Caesar kicked their guns out of reach.

Erin landed a boot in their leader's face. When she reared back and swung at him again, his hand snaked out, hooked her ankle and pulled hard.

She fell backward and hit the floor so hard, her head bounced and the air whooshed out of her lungs.

Her captor rolled on top of her and jammed a knife to her throat. "Move and I kill her."

"Like hell you will," Caesar roared. He grabbed the back of the man's collar and yanked him up off Erin. In one swift swing, he hit him with a hard right to jaw.

The terrorist's head jerked back and he crumpled to the ground.

At that same moment, MPs stormed through the door, weapons pointed at Caesar.

"Halt, or we'll shoot!" One young sergeant shouted.

Erin rolled to her feet and stood in front of Caesar, swaying but holding out her arms. "Don't shoot him. He's one of us." Her head swam and she would have fallen if Caesar hadn't pulled her against him from behind. God, being held in his arms felt good.

Caesar dragged off the ski mask, chuckled and lifted her. "I'm U.S Navy SEAL Caesar Sanchez, a patient at this fine institution."

"Sir, could you put the lieutenant down, please, and step away from her?" the sergeant asked.

Erin wrapped her arms around his neck. "No, he can't. He's saving me."

Caesar kissed her forehead. "No, *mi amor*, you saved me."

The military policeman frowned. "Please, put the female down."

A master sergeant entered the room behind the young MP. "At ease, Sergeant. If the lieutenant says he's one of the good guys, he's probably one of the good guys. You can start processing the ones on the floor."

Erin glanced down at the man who'd held a knife to her throat. "If charges are set all around the hospital, shouldn't we get out of here?"

"They were bluffing," Caesar said, with a definitive head shake.

Her brows rose and her lips quirked on the corners. "And you know this because?"

"I understand just enough Pashto to recognize when one of them corrected the leader saying, We do not have explosives."

"A handy talent to have." She kissed him, nibbling at his lip, so glad he showed up. "Is there anything else I should know about you?"

"That about sums it up." Stepping over the two men he'd knocked out, Caesar carried Erin out into the hallway. "You need to see a doctor."

Sighing, she nestled against his chest. "I've never felt better." Through the throbbing pain in her head and eye, she couldn't remember such a feeling of elation as when she'd recognized Caesar in the terrorist's clothing. "How did you know?"

"I could say that I'm a trouble magnet, and trouble seems to follow you around. But I couldn't sleep and I had to see you."

"So you were wandering around the halls at night in your bare feet?" She trailed a finger down his neck.

"I had on shower shoes, but they made too much noise."

She pressed her cheek against his chest. "Well, I'm glad you couldn't sleep."

"Hey." His grip tightened. "I'm supposed to be a recuperating patient. What kind of nursely thing is that to say?"

"The best."

He swiveled his head in both directions then stared into her eyes. "Aren't you afraid you'll get in trouble for fraternization?"

She shook her head. "I don't care."

"That's new. Is the good, rule-following lieutenant chucking the old rule book?"

She grinned. "As far as I can throw it."

"Good." He kissed her gently on her cracked lips. "What made you change your mind?"

Her smile fading, she looked up into his eyes. "Staring at death in the faces of a few terrorists makes a girl think twice about walking away from a good thing."

"You're not afraid I'll run out, or cheat with another woman?"

"Like you said. That's not your style." She cupped his cheeks in her hands. "Caesar Sanchez, you're a good man, and now you're my hero."

"Now don't go putting me up on a pedestal." He winked. "I might like it too much."

"Don't worry, I can knock you down if I need to."

"That would be all too easy. You hold my heart in the palm of your hand."

"Nice words, Romeo."

"I try." He kissed her forehead. "Where did you learn that eye-poking move?"

"From my dad. When he found out I enlisted into the military, he knew I might need to defend myself from friendly attacks."

"A smart man, looking out for his daughter. A beautiful woman like you gets hit on all the time." He set her on her feet and smoothed the loose hairs out of her face. Then he tugged at the elastic band holding what remained of her ponytail in a drunken list. Her hair swung free and he feathered his hands through its length. "Mmm. I love the way your hair smells like sunshine and lemons."

"I like when you talk sweet to me." She kissed his cheek. "I didn't thank you properly for the roses."

"They were a bribe."

"Whatever they were, they worked." She touched a finger to his chest. "I don't know how this will work, or how long a relationship will last, but I find myself willing to take a few risks where you're concerned." She leaned back her head and stared at him through her good eye and her swollen one, a lopsided smile lifting one corner of her busted lips. "I also find myself in need of a hero and you just happen to fill the bill."

"I'm your man." Caesar swept her up in his arms again.

"Sir, ma'am, do you mind?" The Master Sergeant emerged from the room, wheeling the litter with the prisoner.

"Not at all." Caesar stepped out of the way, still carrying Erin in his arms.

Erin sighed. "You better let me down. Hassani needs to get back to the ICU and hooked up to oxygen."

Caesar lowered her legs to the ground, and held on until she could stand on her own. "Can't you let someone else take over his care?"

"I'm the ICU nurse on duty."

"I'd think that would have ended when you were taken hostage."

She snorted. "Does your duty as a SEAL end when you're not on a mission?" Eyebrows quirked, she crossed her arms. "No. Please. I need to check on Sheila. She was injured in the takeover."

"Okay, but we're not done yet."

"Agreed."

Erin and Caesar entered the elevator with the Master Sergeant and rode up to the third floor where more MPs were cleaning up the other terrorists.

Sheila met them at the door to the ICU, a goose-egg-sized lump marring her forehead along with a big, purple bruise on her jaw. "Oh, thank God, you're all right." She hugged Erin and stepped back to examine her. "You look like hell."

Erin laughed, the pull on her lip making her wince. "You look pretty beat up yourself."

Sheila smiled weakly. "At least we're alive."

"Our other patients?"

"Stable." She led the way into the room Hassani had been assigned. With Caesar and the master sergeant's help, they moved him to the bed.

Erin and Sheila reattached the drainage tubes, oxygen, IVs and electronic monitors. Hassani's blood pressure and pulse were low, but he'd probably survive.

Caesar hung around the nurses' station of the ICU until they emerged.

"You should go back to your hospital bed," Erin said.

"You need to see a doctor."

"I'm fine. I'm on duty for another two hours."

Caesar shook his head. "I'm not going anywhere without you."

"I'm okay with that." She smiled and the last knot of tension in her stomach relaxed. "I feel safer with you around. Sheila?"

"He has my vote." She winked at Caesar. "Let him stay. I'll go so far as to notify his area that he isn't AWOL."

"Would you like to take a seat?" Erin asked.

"If it's all the same to you, I think I'll stand."

"Oh, dear Lord." Erin sucked in a breath and turned. "With everything happening, I forgot about your stitches. Want us to take a look?"

He stepped away, his cheeks reddening, and his hands shot toward his butt. "If it's all the same to you, I'd rather suffer in silence."

"Is the big, Navy SEAL embarrassed?" Erin's lips quirked.

"Hell, yeah," he responded. "Contrary to popular belief, not all SEALs are exhibitionists."

"Sweetie," Sheila said. "Take him into an empty room. I'll cover for you."

"I could kiss you." Caesar gripped the woman by the arms and planted a big kiss on her cheek.

She sputtered, her face bright red. "Well, there's no need for that. But if you insist." Grabbing his arms, she planted a big kiss square on his lips and then stepped back, wiping her hand over her mouth. "If I were only twenty years younger..."

Erin chuckled as she reached into the supply cabinet for gauze and rubbing alcohol. She led Caesar into the closest bathroom, the only room without windows. "This is where I was when the terrorists attacked." She trembled. "I admit, I was pretty scared."

As soon as the door closed behind him, he pulled her into his arms. "You don't have to be scared anymore."

She laughed, her voice shaking. "I know that." Holding the bottle of alcohol and the gauze in front of her like a shield, she delayed the inevitable. "I need to take care of your—"

Caesar cut off her words with a gentle kiss. "Later."

"But—"

He took the bottle of alcohol and the gauze and set them on the sink. "I'm fine and the only thing that could make me better is to hold you in my arms." His hands came up around her waist.

Who was she trying to kid? She wanted to be in his arms and she was tired of fighting the desire. Erin melted against him, resting her hands on his broad chest. "Too bad I arranged to be on a flight to Bagram later today."

"You're injured and security forces will want statements from you on the attack. I'm sure you can postpone." He gripped the zipper on the front of her flight suit and dragged it downward.

Her breath caught and held, her heartbeat racing in anticipation of where this was going. "Think a week will be enough?" she asked, her voice barely above a whisper as his knuckles brushed against her breast, her belly and lower.

"Not nearly." He pushed the suit over her shoulders and slid down her bra straps, freeing her breasts. "But we'll make do." One slow, sweet kiss at a time, he seared a path along the curve of her jaw and the long line of her neck, pausing where her pulse raced at the base of her throat.

How would they make this thing between them work? Because Erin knew in her heart, she wanted it more than anything. "I redeploy in two months back to the States. I'm assigned to Langley Air Force Base."

"Perfect." He bent to take one of her breasts into his mouth and sucked on the nipple. "I'll be back at Little Creek soon."

"We can see each other there without worrying about fraternization rules."

"Mmm." He shifted to the other breast, nudging her flight suit lower with his hands.

The uniform slipped over her hips and down her legs to pool around her boots. "We don't have much time," she said, her words breathy from the excitement of his attention.

"Then we'd better hurry."

Pushing aside her last misgivings about making love in the bathroom while on duty, Erin stepped out of the suit and panties, and stood in her boots.

Caesar's face lit as his gaze swept over her body. "I didn't think you could get any sexier than naked in tennis shoes, but, baby, you're smokin' hot in nothin' but boots." He lifted her, easing her knees around his hips. Then he remembered.

"Fuck."

"Yeah." She chuckled. "That's the idea."

He shook his head. "No condom." He sighed, easing her up off the tip of his cock. "Risking it once was bad. Twice is asking for trouble."

A knock on the door made them both jump.

"Since you're...er...checking his injuries," Sheila said through the heavy door, "you might need one of these."

Caesar opened the door, Erin reached around the edge and Sheila pressed a foil package into her hand.

With a laugh, Erin held up a condom and said, "Bless you, Sheila."

"My pleasure," she responded.

Caesar closed the door. "Remind me to kiss that woman."

"I'm in!" Sheila called out.

"Over my dead body." Erin glared at Caesar. "I thought you were done kissing other women?"

"Everyone but you, mi amor." He pressed his lips against her mouth and slid his tongue inside to tangle with hers.

He tasted like heaven.

When he allowed her to breathe again, she sighed. "That's more like it." Then Erin rolled the condom down over him and smiled. "Now, can a girl get lucky?"

Caesar squeezed her hips. "I thought you'd never ask."

Careful not to disturb his stitches, she sank down over his engorged member.

Grinning, Caesar pressed her back against the door and gently rocked into her, increasing the pace and intensity with each thrust.

With a moan, she gave herself up to him, riding him like the stallion he was, loving how complete she felt in her SEAL's embrace.

If you enjoyed this book, you might enjoy others in the
Take No Prisoners Series:
SEAL's Honor (#1)
SEAL's Ultimate Challenge (#1.5)
SEAL'S Desire (#2)
SEAL's Embrace (#3)
SEAL's Obsession (#4)
SEAL's Proposal (#5)
SEAL's Seduction (#6)
SEAL'S Defiance (#7)
SEAL's Deception (#8)

SEAL'S OBSESSION

TAKE NO PRISONERS SERIES BOOK #4

New York Times & USA Today
Bestselling Author

Elle James

TAKE NO PRISONERS
JACK & NATALIE
BOOK 4

SEAL's
Obsession

New York Times & USA Today Bestselling Author
ELLE JAMES

1

"I wonder what you have to do to retire in a place like this?" Navy SEAL Corpsman Jack Fischer cut the engine on the jet ski, letting it slide across the crystal clear water and up onto the white sands of the beach.

"You have to either belong to a cartel or pay the cartel to protect you," said a voice through the earbud. Swede, the computer guru and all-around electronic techie on SEAL Team 10, kept them connected through comm equipment.

"Just remember, Fish, we're not here on vacation." Gator's gruff voice rattled in Jack's ear. Remy had been on SEAL Team 10 longer than Jack and had seen a lot more action. He'd taken Jack under his wing on his first day in the unit.

"It's hard to keep that in mind when the water's so

clear I can see fifty feet down. I'd rather bust out my scuba gear and do some recreational diving." Jack adjusted his sunglasses. "You sure there's not some old abandoned shipwreck we can't blow up close by?"

"Save it for when we nail the pirates who've been stealing boats around here," Gator said. "No doubt we'll have plenty of action and opportunities to blow up shit."

Jack stared out at serene blue waters along the coastline of Honduras. As smooth and calm as the bay was, this area had seen its share of trouble. In the past month, four expensive pleasure yachts had been hijacked and disappeared. Their rich owners had been taken hostage by leftist guerillas operating under the name Castillo Commando. Most of the hostages had been ransomed and released, their ransom dollars used to fund the guerilla activities.

In the latest attack, they'd stolen a yacht owned by wealthy American business owner William Bentley and his nephew. His high-powered political contacts included the Secretary of Defense, who called in the Navy SEALs to locate and recover the missing hostages and eliminate the leftist guerrilla pirates from the Honduran coastline.

Jack, along with a twenty-two-man team from SEAL Team 10, had been deployed to handle the mission labeled Operation Constrictor.

They'd located the scuttled yachts in a nearby

island inlet, but hadn't found the hideout of the Castillo Commando. Their only lead was a few satellite images of a couple of boats landing on the bay of Trujillo around midnight the day Bentley disappeared.

The Secretary of Defense, along with Bentley's wife, secured another yacht to use as a decoy loaded with Navy SEALs and complex intelligence-gathering equipment to help them recover the missing yacht owners and eradicate the guerrilla pirates. Four days had passed and no pirates had come or gone from the shores of the bay. They hadn't taken the bait or even come out to sniff around.

"Some vacation, huh?" Jack said as he strolled along the beach, collecting seashells.

"At least you're on the beach with half a chance of seeing women in bikinis," Swede grumbled.

"All we have here are some kids playing and old men in fishing boats." Jack stopped on the sand and performed a three-hundred-sixty-degree turn. In one direction were the old men and fishing boats. In the other was an empty skiff dragged up on the shore.

Jack lifted his hand to shade his eyes from the sun sinking lower over the jungle. At the edge of the sand in the shade of the jungle was a small gathering of dark-skinned locals. They seemed to be crowding around a group set up under a tent awning.

Curious, Jack set off across the sand to check it out, feeling a little naked without his combat gear or even a weapon as part of his attempt to appear as a bored, rich young man looking for something to do. Because he had the fewest tattoos of his SEAL brothers and he rocked a California surfer look that usually captured attention, he'd been chosen as the lure.

As he neared the gathering, he heard a voice call out in Spanish, "Please, wait your turn."

Standing at the edge of the gathering, Jack noted a woman holding a child with a skin rash over his belly. Another woman held a little girl with long black hair who cried softly against her mother's breast. A long jagged gash in her leg looked like it wasn't healing properly.

A narrow gap opened in the throng, giving Jack a view of the focus of the locals' attention. Three men and two women wearing scrubs sat on campstools with a folding table between them. One by one, they examined each patient, cleaning wounds, stitching lacerations and prescribing cleaning techniques. Some of the patients received shots, others pills, but they were all treated with a smile and gentle words and gestures.

A bald man in scrubs led a woman and a small child to a pretty medical worker with light brown hair and green eyes. She wore green scrubs and had her hair pulled back in a messy bun with tendrils falling around her cheeks.

"Dr. Rhoades," the man said in English. "This child needs your attention."

The woman smiled at the dark-eyed little girl who limped toward her followed by an older woman. When they got close, the child buried her face in the old woman's skirt, crying.

The older woman spoke in rapid Spanish. "My granddaughter was bitten by a spider. Her leg is swollen and painful, and she is frightened of the doctor, afraid she will take her away from her family."

Smiling, the woman with the soft brown hair and gentle face rose from the campstool and dropped to her knees in the sand, putting herself on eye-level with the little girl. She spoke quietly in halting Spanish, smiling gently.

Jack couldn't hear her words, but he fell under her spell just as easily as the child.

The little girl nodded.

Dr. Rhoades spoke again.

The child and her grandmother both laughed.

When the doctor held out her hand, the little girl took it and allowed the doctor draw her onto her lap. She let the child listen to her own heartbeat through her stethoscope before she listened. Then she set the girl on the table beside her and examined her leg. By the time she'd cleaned and bandaged the leg, the little girl was smiling. Then she and her grandmother both hugged her and thanked her for helping them.

As Jack watched the line of locals slowly dissipate, he noticed the sun had slipped lower in the sky, making the shadows thicken on the edge of the trees. A shout caught his attention, drawing it away from the medical team.

Pushing his way through the remaining patients, a scrawny teenager spoke, waving his hands toward a dirt road. He grabbed a woman's arm and dragged her in the opposite direction. He let go and took another's hand and pulled her along, leading her away from the medical team and the dirt road that had him so upset. He turned back and ran toward the doctor, shouting hysterically.

Jack stiffened and glanced around, realizing he'd zoned out while watching Dr. Rhoades work with her patients. To keep the teen from reaching the doctor, Jack stepped in front of him.

The boy tried to dodge him.

Jack grabbed his arms.

The teen shouted something in Spanish but he was so distraught, Jack had a hard time understanding him. Two words stood out in the rest of his hysterical shouts. Castillo Commando.

Jack stiffened.

As if someone pulled the plug on a sink, the remaining locals disappeared into the trees.

Frantic, the boy twisted until he broke loose of Jack's hold and raced into the trees.

The doctor and the others wearing scrubs quickly packed their medical kits, folded tables and chairs and hurried toward the boat on the beach, glancing back over their shoulders.

"What's going on, Fish?" Gator spoke in his ear.

"Not sure, but I think the Commandos are coming." He stared at the shadowy woods, shocked not a single local could be seen. If he hadn't observed them for himself, he would have thought the beach had always been deserted.

The sound of gunfire from the dirt road at the far end of the beach jerked his attention to the north. A truck sped toward the medical personnel.

Jack bolted for the jet ski. His gaze shot to the doctor's small group.

One man dropped back to get behind the female doctor. No sooner had he let her go ahead of him, he jerked and grabbed his leg. He dropped the chair he'd been holding and limped as fast as he could, leaving a trail of blood in the sand. The rest of the crew ran across the sand to the little boat and threw in the chairs and tables. They turned and helped the injured man into the boat and then pushed off as, one by one, they jumped in, landing at odd angles.

The doctor and the bald guy were the last to climb aboard and the water was getting deep.

"Go! Go! Go!" The bald guy yelled as he pointed toward the open water.

Dr. Rhoades dragged herself over the side of the boat and fell into the bottom.

The tattooed bald man jumped in, and all of them ducked low as bullets pelted the water around them.

From a crouch, Jack shoved the jet ski across the sand and into the water, hitting the start button. The engine stuttered. "Start, dammit!" He hit the button again and the engine roared to life. Gunning the throttle, he rocketed out into the bay, laying low over the machine.

"What's going on, Fish?" Swede demanded.

"We're under attack. I'd say we found our guerillas." Jack swung wide to follow the little boat chugging toward a larger one, it's side marked with a big red cross, anchored in the bay. They'd almost reached it when a jet boat, equipped with a mounted machinegun and a dozen armed men rounded the spit at the edge of the bay, barreling toward the ship. The skiff filled with medical personnel barely slid alongside the bigger boat as the attackers opened fire.

"Shit!" Jack called out, feeling helpless and outgunned.

"A little intel would help, Jack," Swede prompted.

"A fully-armed gun boat is heading toward what I suspect is a floating medical boat in the bay here. I could use some air support about now."

"Scrambling the Black Hawk. ETA ten mikes."

His body tensed. "There won't be anything left in ten minutes."

"Hold that thought." Swede went silent for a few

precious seconds and came back on. "It's your lucky day. The Black Hawk is airborne. The fact they got restless is working in your favor. ETA five minutes. Think you can hold off the guerillas for that long?"

"Sure. No weapons and nothing but a jet ski?" Jack snorted. "I've got this."

"We have a boat on the way, ETA five mikes."

Jack kept heading for the medical boat. As he neared, he noted all hands were on deck to secure the skiff and get the bigger boat underway. Only one man stood on deck with a handgun. The weapon would be too little too late once the machine gun came within range.

He had to do something. Turning away from the big medical boat, he steered toward the fully-equipped gunboat. One unarmed man in nothing but swim trunks, riding a jet ski against a boatload of guerillas. The odds didn't look good, but when did a SEAL run from a challenge? The only easy day was yesterday.

He aimed dead center of the bow, knowing the placement of the machinegun would be most effective off the port or starboard. As long as none of the guerillas moved forward with their rifles, Jack might get close enough to...

Hell if he knew. This wasn't one of those carefully crafted operations where the team practiced every move from start to finish in mockups of their target. This was ad-lib, and he was going it alone. No one had his six, or laid down supporting fire to keep the bad guys occupied long enough for him to close the distance.

As he neared the gunboat, he spotted three guerillas moving to the front, bringing their weapons to their shoulders.

So much for the element of surprise.

Jack zigzagged as he closed on the boat and dodged to the right, leaning hard to create a large rooster tail of a splash, drenching the armed men. Unfortunately, the turn placed him on the starboard side of the gunboat, giving the machine gunner a perfect target.

Bullets pelted the water all around him as he zigzagged across the ocean's surface. One clipped his thigh, tearing through his favorite swim trunks. Well, damn.

"Come on, air support!" he yelled, throttle wide open as he led the gunboat away from the craft the doctor and her staff had boarded and set underway.

With the roar of the jet ski in his ears, he didn't hear the Black Hawk until he saw it swoop in and strafe the gunboat with fifty-caliber bullets.

Dr. Natalie Rhoades hovered on the deck of the Nightingale, watching as the man on the jet ski headed straight for the guerilla gunship, her heart lodged in her throat. "Is that guy insane?"

"He's buying us time to get away," Mac Pennington,

a bald, tattooed combat medic, stood at her side, shaking his head. "And yes, he's insane."

The drumbeat of helicopter rotors filled the air as a Black Hawk helicopter popped over the shoreline trees and headed straight for the gunboat.

Hallie Kristofer joined Natalie and Mac, clapping her hands. "Yay! The cavalry has arrived!"

The machine gunners abandoned their attack on the man on the jet ski and focused on the helicopter.

With the Black Hawk keeping the gunboat full of leftist guerillas engaged, the jet ski turned toward their boat. They had barely gotten underway when he caught up to them.

"We have a visitor, Skipper!" Mac shouted.

"Should we stop?" Hallie asked.

Natalie gripped the rail. "Yes, of course. He saved us from the guerillas, the least we can do is bring him on board and thank him properly."

"Steve and the Skipper are the only ones with guns on the boat." Mac stretched to look overboard toward the rider. "Skipper has to drive the boat, and with Steve out of commission due to the gunshot wound, should I get his gun?"

"No, I saw this man on the shore," Natalie said. "He looked pretty harmless." She was stretching it by saying he looked harmless. Unarmed would have been a better description. The man was big, like he worked out...a lot. He didn't have a spare ounce of flesh on his body and the tattoos on his shoulders and back gave him a motorcycle rider, bad-boy appearance. But those clear blue eyes and shaggy blond hair softened that image. He could have been any beach bum off the coast of California. Either way, he'd made more of an impression on her than she cared to admit.

"Looks can be deceiving," Hallie warned with a frown.

Natalie nodded. "But he risked his life and saved us from attack. We have to give him the benefit of a doubt."

"I'll go help Daphne and Jean-David," Mac said. "Just to be sure."

"I'm coming, too," Natalie said. "We'll go under the assumption that there is safety in numbers."

A shout rose up from the back of the boat, "Throw me a line!"

The boat slowed. Ship's deckhand, Daphne Bradford, tossed the man a line off the back.

He grabbed it and dragged himself and the jet ski up to tie onto the dinghy at the rear. Jean-David and Mac both held out their hands to help him on board.

The jet ski rider grabbed one of each and let them haul him onboard.

Hallie turned and shouted toward the pilot house, "Go!"

The engine engaged and the Nightingale sped

away from the gunboat that was still taking fire from the Black Hawk.

Natalie stepped forward, her pulse kicking up as she faced the man with all the muscles. Up close, he was much larger than when he'd been standing on the edge of the crowd of women and children on shore.

"Who's in charge?" he asked, scanning the three on deck.

Her knees wobbling more than they should have, Natalie stepped forward. "I am. Welcome aboard the Nightingale. Thank you for saving us from the guerillas." She held out her hand.

He took it in his, those blue eyes shining as she gave it a firm shake.

"I'm Jack Fischer. Thanks for letting me come on board. My jet ski was getting low on fuel. I wasn't sure I'd make it back to my boat. How's the guy who got shot?"

Hallie answered before Natalie could. "Dr. Biacowski is working with him now."

Natalie had taken a cursory look at the wound. "He should be okay, barring any infection." She glanced around the end of the bay. "What boat did you say you came from?"

"I'm with some buddies of mine on the Pegasus." Jack pointed to a large pleasure yacht anchored near the southern end of the large bay.

Even from a distance, Natalie could see the

gleaming white hull of the craft. She glanced back at Jack. He didn't quite fit the image she had of a rich yacht owner on vacation.

His lips quirked and he stared down at his naked torso with the tattoos and his torn shorts. "I'm working for my passage aboard the yacht."

Blood dripped off the bottom hem of Jack's black swim trunks onto the white deck.

"You're bleeding!" Hallie hooked his arm and led him toward a bench. "Come over here and sit down. Mac, could you get Dr. Rhoades's bag?"

"It's right here. I've got it." Natalie grabbed her satchel from where it landed when they transferred from the dinghy. She'd been content to stand back and let Hallie and Mac do all the talking, but with an injury at hand, her natural instinct was to heal.

Hallie pushed Jack onto a bench. "If you'll hand me the scissors, I'll cut away the fabric."

Natalie pulled her surgical scissors from the bag. "No need. I can do this," she told her nurse.

Hallie moved away, giving Natalie room to kneel in front of Jack. When she raised her scissors to cut away the fabric, Jack jerked his leg out of range.

"I happen to like these swim trunks. If it's all the same to you, I can pull them up." A grin spread across his face. "Unless you want me to take them off."

Natalie's eyes widened and her breath caught in her throat. He was practically naked already and she was breathless. She was afraid she'd pass out if he were completely nude. Mentally chastising herself, she focused on the injury, not the man. Hell, she'd seen naked women, children and men. Jack Fischer was no different. Every body had much the same characteristics.

Jack just had more in all the right places.

Heat rose up her neck and suffused her cheeks at that errant thought. "Just pull it up," she said, her voice squeaking, causing the heat in her cheeks to intensify.

"Wow," Hallie said. "You've got some powerful thighs."

"Hallie!" Dr. Rhoades snapped, not so much because of the inappropriateness of her statement, but because she'd been thinking it herself. "Put your tongue back in your head and hand me some gauze and alcohol."

Hallie winked at Jack. "Your shoulders are anatomically exceptional, as well." She opened the bottle of alcohol and handed it and the gauze to Natalie. "Is that better?" she asked, batting her eyelashes.

Mac snorted. "Seriously, Hallie?"

Natalie tipped the bottle of alcohol over the gauze. "He's a patient, not an entertainer at a strip club."

Jack's sudden bark of laughter startled Natalie and she spilled alcohol onto his leg, some of which found its way into his wound. His laughter turned into a slight hiss. "God, that feels good," he said through gritted teeth.

"Good Lord," Hallie muttered. "He even makes pain look sexy."

"He's just a guy. A beach bum," Mac noted.

"I'm employed," Jack corrected, his eyes gleaming with mischief. "I gave up being a bum for a paycheck and a chance to see the world, one exotic port at a time."

Natalie couldn't help but get caught up in Jack's rich, deep tone and playful expression. Pushing back her shoulders, she applied the soaked gauze to his wound.

This time he didn't flinch, his gaze on hers as she held the gauze with a firm touch, gauging his tolerance for pain. Then she cleaned the area and held out her hand. "Dry gauze, please."

Hallie handed Natalie more gauze. "Sounds romantic." She sighed. "So, Jack, do you have a girl in every port?"

"Hallie!" Natalie clapped the gauze over the injury a little harder than she would have liked.

Jack smiled, his jaw tight. "Are you this gentle with all your patients, Dr. Rhoades?"

"Ignore Hallie," Mac said with a shake of his head. "She's been cooped up on the boat too long. I think she needs a night out."

Hallie crossed her arms over her chest, her chin

lifting in challenge. "You're right. I could use a night out." Her mouth curled into a saucy grin. "But it would be so much better if the night was with Jack."

Mac's jaw tightened. "I see." He turned toward Natalie. "Do you need me for anything, Dr. Rhoades?"

She glanced at his taut face and almost asked him what was wrong, but Mac looked like he could bite the cap off a bottle of beer with his teeth. "No, thank you. Perhaps Dr. Biacowski could use your skills with Steve. I'm worried he hasn't come up from below."

"I'll check." Mac turned on his heels and stalked away.

Natalie waited until Mac had disappeared below deck until she said, "Hallie, I'd like for you to go, too."

"But you don't have anyone here to assist you."

"I can manage Mr. Fischer's wound care on my own now, thank you."

"What if he's working with the guerillas and attacks you?"

Natalie glanced up into eyes a beautiful shade of blue and she gulped. "Mr. Fischer, are you going to attack me?"

He hesitated, his eyes flaring. Then he shook his head. "Not unless you want me to."

Hallie choked on her laughter. "I knew he was a bad boy. He has it written all over him."

"Hallie," Natalie warned, though, at times, she wished she could be as direct as Hallie. The younger woman had nailed it—the man had bad boy written all over every inch of his incredible body.

"What?" Hallie raised her hands. "I can't help that I worry about you."

"Daphne and Jean-David are on deck. If I need assistance, I can call out to them." Natalie tipped her head toward the door.

"I'm going." Hallie's lips firmed into a tight line. "Though the view is much better out here than in the cabin." She left, glancing over her shoulder one last time before she disappeared through the cabin door.

Tearing adhesive tape from a roll, Natalie secured the gauze to Jack's thick, tanned thigh, her fingers pressing into the solid muscle. She pressed the adhesive several times to be sure it stuck—not that she was gauging the hardness of his muscle. He smelled of sun and salt water, and his shoulders were so broad they blocked the light from the setting sun from glaring into her eyes.

"Nice work, doc." He stood and pulled her to her feet.

She stood so close, she felt the heat radiating off his body and had to fight the urge to touch him.

The boat rocked in the waves and she fell against that hard, muscular chest, her palms planting against the smooth, taut plains.

His arm came up around her waist, clamping her

against him, her hips firmly pressed against his. "I've got you," he assured her.

His soothing tones did nothing to slow her racing pulse. Boy did he, with strong arms and a rock-solid body. Natalie's body lit up like a furnace.

"So, what's the prognosis, doc?"

His lips were so close she could feel the warmth of his breath. "Prognosis?" she whispered. All coherent thought escaped her as she curled her fingers into his skin.

"Will I live?" he asked.

"I don't know." She shifted her gaze up to his eyes and fell into the deep blue orbs. "It's too soon to tell."

"Perhaps this will help you decide." He bent to brush his lips lightly over hers.

Normally one to hold every man at arm's length, Natalie didn't protest. She was powerless to resist as his kiss grew more insistent and he claimed her mouth.

When he allowed her up for air, she stared into his eyes.

The boat shifted again and her bag slid across the deck, bumping into the backs of her ankles, returning her to her senses. "Let go of me."

Jack's eyes narrowed, his brows drawing together. "My apologies for being so forward." He dropped his arm from around her waist and stepped back.

Natalie immediately missed the warmth of his embrace, but she couldn't let him kiss her again. She had a strict personal code of not fooling around with the crewmembers.

A tiny voice in her head reminded her he wasn't a member of her crew.

Either way, she wasn't interested in getting involved with any man. She'd already had one good marriage with a man she loved. She doubted seriously she could be so fortunate as to find another man who could rise to that level. "I'll have Skipper bring you close enough to your boat to get there by jet ski. I think it best if you leave, now."

ABOUT THE AUTHOR

ELLE JAMES also writing as MYLA JACKSON is a *New York Times* and *USA Today* Bestselling author of books including cowboys, intrigues and paranormal adventures that keep her readers on the edges of their seats. When she's not at her computer, she's traveling, snow skiing, boating, or riding her ATV, dreaming up new stories. Learn more about Elle James at www.elle-james.com

Website | Blog | Facebook | Twitter | GoodReads | Newsletter
Or visit her alter ego Myla Jackson at mylajackson.com

Website | Blog | Facebook | Twitter | Newsletter

www.ellejames.com
ellejames@ellejames.com

ALSO BY ELLE JAMES

Smoldering Desire (#3)

Hellfire in High Heels (#4)

Playing With Fire (#5)

Up in Flames (#6) TBD

Total Meltdown (#7) TBD

Mission: Six

One Intrepid SEAL

Two Dauntless Hearts

Three Courageous Words

Four Relentless Days

Five Ways to Surrender

Six Minutes to Midnight

Hearts & Heroes Series

Wyatt's War (#1)

Mack's Witness (#2)

Ronin's Return (#3)

Sam's Surrender (#4)

Take No Prisoners Series

SEAL's Honor (#1)

SEAL'S Desire (#2)

SEAL's Embrace (#3)

Cajun Magic Mysteries Books 1-3

Billionaire Online Dating Service

The Billionaire Husband Test (#1)

The Billionaire Cinderella Test (#2)

The Billionaire Bride Test (#3) TBD

The Billionaire Matchmaker Test (#4) TBD

SEAL Of My Own

Navy SEAL Survival

Navy SEAL Captive

Navy SEAL To Die For

Navy SEAL Six Pack

Devil's Shroud Series

Deadly Reckoning (#1)

Deadly Engagement (#2)

Deadly Liaisons (#3)

Deadly Allure (#4)

Deadly Obsession (#5)

Deadly Fall (#6)

Covert Cowboys Inc Series

Triggered (#1)

Taking Aim (#2)

Bodyguard Under Fire (#3)

Cowboy Resurrected (#4)

Navy SEAL Justice (#5)

Navy SEAL Newlywed (#6)

High Country Hideout (#7)

Clandestine Christmas (#8)

Thunder Horse Series

Hostage to Thunder Horse (#1)

Thunder Horse Heritage (#2)

Thunder Horse Redemption (#3)

Christmas at Thunder Horse Ranch (#4)

Demon Series

Hot Demon Nights (#1)

Demon's Embrace (#2)

Tempting the Demon (#3)

Lords of the Underworld

Witch's Initiation (#1)

Witch's Seduction (#2)

The Witch's Desire (#3)

Possessing the Witch (#4)

Stealth Operations Specialists (SOS)

Nick of Time

Alaskan Fantasy

Blown Away

Warrior's Conquest

Rogues

Enslaved by the Viking Short Story

Conquests

Smokin' Hot Firemen

Love on the Rocks

Protecting the Colton Bride

Heir to Murder

Secret Service Rescue

High Octane Heroes

Haunted

Engaged with the Boss

Cowboy Brigade

Time Raiders: The Whisper

Bundle of Trouble

Killer Body

Operation XOXO

An Unexpected Clue

Baby Bling

Made in the USA
Columbia, SC
27 July 2022